MURDER UNDER THE WAX MYRTLES

A WARM SPRINGS MYSTERY
BOOK ONE

D. SMITH

Murder Under the Wax Myrtles by D. Smith

Published by Kingfisher Press

Fairview, North Carolina, United States of America

Visit the author's website at www.douglaspsmith.com

Cover design by Getcovers

Print ISBN: 978-1-964344-03-4

CHAPTER ONE

The sweet spring day ended in a pleasant sunset, the soft breeze carrying the scent of early flowers. I had eaten a nice dinner and now sat in my comfortable leather chair. Kat was stretched on her back by my side, filling the spot between me and the arm of the chair. It was just big enough for her. We had spent many nights like this over the past few months. I looked around at all the architectural detail and woodwork of the old cottage and again thought how well built and decorated the homes were on the Roosevelt campus in Warm Springs, abbreviated as the RWS campus. Sometime later, while reading, I dozed off.

I woke in the dark, muddle-headed but quickly realizing this was my regular period of sleepless anxiety for some time now. Kat had gone to look out the window at the night creatures in the yard. There was enough light filtering through curtains to make out most of the room's details. Including the bottle on the shelf.

I stared at the bottle and for a brief second. I wanted to go over and pick it up. But I knew it would not help. So, I did not move either. Stalemate. The bottle had been there, unopened, for months. I knew what false promise it held. My troubles would be over if I just took it up and emptied the amber contents into my body, soothing my soul for a brief time. Each night, I made a decision not to open the bottle, using it as motivation to be thankful for my mostly good life.

Standing up, I kicked off my slippers and slid into my shoes. It was time to wander about and make like the ghost I was worried about becoming. Leaving the house and entering the bright night, lit up from the security lights on campus. I understood the concept of keeping students safe, but I wanted to walk in the dark. It was more intimate and enjoyable to be part of the night in a way not possible in the daytime. Every night I had the choice of the sidewalk or the street. There was no difference in car traffic between the two. That was a testament to the amount of vehicular traffic on campus at night, which was exactly none. I chose the street.

Soon I left campus proper and the harsh lights. Moving quietly in my stealth shoes, I began the slow uphill loop. The night was redolent with the fragrance of several flowers. I had been here long enough to know each turn of the warm season held its different scents. Early spring was heavy with wisteria and daffodils. Later spring with azaleas and the sweetly cloying smell of invasive Japanese privet.

Summer brought magnolia with the bouquet of heavy citrus creams, often mixed with heavenly gardenia. Even winter held its own with the scent of camellias if you were close enough. Any time of year the breeze could carry notes of cedar or pine.

Quickly my mood rose, and I enjoyed the night. Late night outside provided a kind of solace, my head clearing from being in nature with no people around, smelling what the earth brought forth and hearing the cacophony of the insects. And night birds once the whippoorwills started.

And of course, the sound of trains. Always the trains. The lifeblood of the South, and scourge of the insomniacs. But even the train sounds were comforting in a way. A reminder there was a bigger world out there, mine again if I decided to leave this place. Yet each day, I decided to stay and enjoy what I had, especially because I still had a lot to be thankful for.

Getting here was an interesting journey. But then, that is true for anybody in the world getting to anywhere. We are all at any moment just the latest result of all the decisions, bad and good, we've made for years. Or non-decisions. But here we are anyway. And here I was in Warm Springs, Georgia, in a lovely old cottage on a beautiful forgotten campus, in a life designed and planned for two. But I was here alone. I would make the best of it until I decided not to.

Emma and I had been together for a long time. We moved a lot because of my job, and we were both vagabonds at heart. There was always a new adventure in a new land, whether in America or overseas. With age came the desire to find something more stable. Asheville seemed like a good fit for a while. But a freak hurricane ruined that dream, so we looked for a place not only stable, but safe. Those two parameters we found more important than fun at this stage of life. We found what we were looking for on America's most underrated campus in Warm Springs. Underrated because probably a hundred people in the world knew it existed.

But then she had the audacity to die. There was somewhat more to it than that. But talking or thinking about it never made it better. I moved here bringing only furniture and Kat.

I spelled Kat with a K. I was not so droll as to name her Cat with a C. She was possibly a Maine Coon Cat, but nobody believed me. Most of the time, I did not believe it either. Not that she was offended. She was a cat after all, diffident and aloof. The lack of believability stemmed from her size. She weighed eight pounds after dinner. Everyone thinks Maines must be twenty pounds or bigger. But genetics loves its little tricks and especially proving internet experts wrong. She had all the traits of a Maine otherwise. I rarely told anybody she was a Maine anymore to save the arguments. I now said her breed was Finlandic Bog Aggressicattus. Funny how no one argued because they didn't want to admit they didn't know what it was. Once again, Kat didn't care what I told people she was. She was a cat, or rather The Kat.

Lately, she had been learning all the new critters that inhabited the campus. Past years she spent her days outside in Asheville, haphazardly chasing chipmunks and lazing in the sun. Nights she spent with her nose scrunched against the window. She used to watch the bears and raccoons in the yard in Asheville. Now she did the same thing, but it was armadillos, deer and possums parading through the yard. As far as I knew, she had not encountered the substantial fire ant population, but I kept an eye on her. With her thick fur, she could pick up a whole load of them and not even realize it until they all stung her at once. I worried about that, so I tried to control the ant population. It was a losing battle.

Kat loved to find dirt or sand patches and roll in them. I was afraid she might try that on a huge ant mound. But so far not, and I thought perhaps she could smell the ants. They stank of formic acid if you were unlucky enough to get that close to them. I knew Kat was a smart girl so that eased my worry. In Asheville, she always steered clear of the ubiquitous centipedes and millipedes.

She still chased chipmunks around, but the population was smaller here. If she caught one I rescued it, otherwise she would bring it in the house to play with it. Birds interested her, but she rarely had the urge to chase one. I think she knew they were fast and therefore she would not risk the scene of chasing one and not catching it. She also watched the squirrels. But the size of those on campus convinced her not to tangle with them.

Her sum of existence was to get me to feed her a few times a day, open the front door for her, and occasionally rub her belly for fifteen minutes. Her role in my life was to keep me alive. I was responsible for feeding her, after all. Whatever I did for her was immeasurably less than what she did for me. We had an understanding.

All those thoughts and more flitted around on my long walk. Calm now, I made my home. I waved as the police

SUV passed. I was likely the only person they saw at night. Every hour they passed by at least twice, so I guess there was some traffic at night. But no cars from the outside world. I really was lucky in many ways.

Kat mobbed me when I got back. She needed a late-night snack, so we shared a piece of roast chicken. She was somewhat of a food snob. I forgave her for that, and she ignored my habit of being human. After she ate she demanded and received a belly rub. I carried her to bed where she bathed herself then slept by my feet. Still not sleepy, I thought of the house and projects yet to be done.

My house was built in a southern cottage style. White siding with green shutters framing the large windows. Lots of windows. An A-frame-covered front porch slightly reminiscent of a Victorian look. Inside it was original heart of pine floors. They looked good to be a hundred years old. The kitchen was weirdly cut up since old kitchens were quite different than more modern designs. I wondered about those differences until I visited the Little White House. I'd been there several times, but that time I visited with a purpose. It was to observe and photograph elements like the kitchen layout and fireplace design. The weirdly cut up kitchen layout looked a lot like mine, and the farm-style ceramic sink was identical. The layout was the style of the day, based on smaller stoves, ice boxes, and very little counter surface. Somehow people didn't starve or go on strike for better kitchen designs, so I guess it worked for the times. I could adjust as well.

My upstairs was finished space that used to be the tall attic. I put a desk and bookcases to create a study. There were already built-in bookcases so I could have all my books in one place. A younger me had maintained a substantial library. But I divested much of it since I migrated to digital books. Lately though, I was back to collecting physical books, since they didn't expire if I stopped paying for a subscription.

There was a simple basement underneath for storage. The cottage did have one unusual element. An elevator was built into the rear of the house. It no longer worked so I didn't know what to do with it. The backyard hosted a guest cottage of just under four hundred square feet. Completely livable in the past, with a kitchen, full bath, bedroom, and living area. But that was before the termites moved in, and now repairs were my current project. Well, that and the yard.

The abundant deer population had already changed my plans on what kind of garden I would start once the guest cottage was finished. Everything I planted had to be deer resistant. To date my gardens were beds of herbs up front where there was full sun. Deer didn't like the herbs I grew, which was good because I used them for cooking.

I drifted off still thinking about gardens and what next to plant. As always, I dreamed, but I never could quite recall the plot details in the morning. At least I didn't have nightmares. The morning sun poured in the windows as there were no close trees on the east side of the house.

CHAPTER TWO

Showered and dressed, I walked to the cafeteria for coffee. Part of the RWS campus allure was having the cafeteria a hundred yards from my front door. Open every day of the year as far as I knew, it drew the few people on campus in. I usually made my own espresso each morning at home to get the caffeine flowing. But in an effort to minimize my natural isolationist tendencies, coffee at the cafeteria was a must. Rarely crowded, it was an easy place to meet the campus people and local Warm Springs residents. Small town gossip was easy to gather. I had little to contribute but once people learned I was a resident, I always had the pleasure of listening to their stories about their time and experiences on campus. The place was literally dripping with the history of famous and not-so-famous people, and almost none of the stories had been recorded.

My short walk brought me to the Georgia Hall, a rambling building with many purposes. It housed offices, an unused post office, auditorium, ballroom, and other administrative functions. My target was the cafeteria. Upon entering I saw George. Not unusual as he was always there. He was a big man but moved easily. At least six-four in height he had the build to be a bouncer. His demeanor was more like that of a gardener. Our first talk months ago still stuck in my head. The first morning I arrived on campus, I introduced myself to the first person I saw, and he told me his name was George.

"George are you from around here?"

"Yeah, just about like everyone else working here."

"You didn't want to leave and find somewhere else?"

"Oh I left alright. The very day I was old enough."

"Where did you go?"

"A few places, but settled in Atlanta. Came back here when the folks got sick."

"I guess that happens a lot."

"It does. They both worked the cotton mills, then the textile place until they all closed. Owners moved everything out of the country for cheaper labor, so they said. My folks, all they had was the house. A few hundred a month from the government. Medicare took care of some things, but not much for home health care."

"I imagine they didn't want to go to assisted living."

"No, those places, at least the ones we could afford, are

hell holes. Even then they did not get enough to pay for it, so the house would have gone. Just easier for me to come back."

"Are they still around?"

"Nah, they both passed. I stayed because I got the house and now have no payment. I can make enough here for the bills and don't have to chase the rats in Atlanta. Sometimes I miss it, but life is easier here. I can always drive an hour and a half to see it when I want to."

"It definitely is easier here."

"Yes, it is. How did you get here?"

"Had a few members of extended family in the area. Mainly trying to get away from my old life and its ghosts. Looking for quiet and found it here."

"We are all trying to get away from something. But it never quite works out that way, does it?"

"No, it really does not."

Each morning since then George and I traded pleasantries and light gossip. Two days later, my third day on campus, I had met another man that was a regular. I noticed he was older than me and wore a suit most days. Very likely one of the people running the hospital or one of the other departments on campus. One day we sat together and talked. His name was Ison Carlton and he was an administrator for the facility. My guess about his role was right.

"Noticed you and George seem friendly," Ison began.

"Yeah, he seems like a decent guy."

"He is. George was an executive chef at the Four Seasons and Ritz-Carlton in downtown Atlanta. He gave it up to come down here and handle his parents. Probably a good thing, too. He looked like hell when he first came back. His parents were not easy to deal with, but Atlanta was killing him."

"I had no idea."

"Most people don't. You would be surprised at the histories of some of the people around here. A lot went away, and some made it big but still came back."

"Coming home, I guess."

"Yes. Now you, for example, are not exactly from here, but now you are. You never talk about what you used to be, but I doubt it was something simple."

"The short story is I worked for some big companies, and some big universities. Gave me the opportunity to travel the world. Now I'm here looking for a quiet place to be."

"See, I bet there is a lot more in the long version. And not much that is simple."

"I don't know, I have not done much worth talking about."

"Sure, sure. You're just a regular guy looking for some quiet time."

"That's me."

He shook his head with a sardonic grin. He didn't believe anything I said. But I wasn't in a mood to spend hours on the truth. And I didn't think I ever would be. Time to change the subject.

"Is George the reason the food is good even though it's a cafeteria?" I asked.

He saw right through my deflection but played along. "Something like that. Every year the state budgets less money, and there aren't enough regular customers to make up the difference. All that leaves is George putting lip gloss on a hamster."

"I thought it was lipstick on a hog."

"Can't afford either lipstick or a hog around here. George does what he can with what he has."

"I get it. You know, there a is a lot of vacant land on campus. Appears to be lots of cheap labor, too."

"Now that is a good idea. One that will get you in trouble right quick."

"How's that?"

"First of all, if you suggest it, you'll get put in charge. Second, that would play hell with the state accountants trying to control everything. They would not like it."

"I get the first reason it's a bad idea. But thinking about the second almost makes me want to do it."

"There is a place in this world for making spite against the machine. When are you going to start working on it?"

"No time like the present. Who do I need to see to get it going?"

"Well, that would be me. Congratulations on the position of campus garden director. Volunteer, of course. Seems like you've done this before, going around the system."

"More than once, I tried to get some important work done. One time it involved a simple project working with pathogens and animals. From the results, we could devise countermeasures to improve the health of animals and keep both farmers and the food safe."

"Guess somebody didn't like the idea."

"Neither the faculty nor the department head agreed. Then they got the college dean to quash it."

"But you did it anyway."

"Yep. Went around and above them to the university and got it approved without any problem. Probably because it brought in research dollars."

"Obviously, you know how to piss off a bunch of people you work with, including your boss."

"It's a gift. I've done the same with the Agriculture Commissioner for a different state. Another time the entire state legislature and university administration at yet a different state. And something similar with the federal government."

"You're right, you have a talent. Can't quite call that a gift. Although, getting banned from university reemployment in three states might be a gift."

That was interesting. Not many people knew that part of my history. Ison had been checking up on me.

"I like to think it is a gift."

"I knew it."

"What?"

"Goes back to the earlier conversation. You aren't simple at all. More like chaos waiting to happen, in a quiet package."

"Thanks."

I was still working on the community or campus garden concept. But it looked like something that we could start this coming growing season. Two sites had been picked, one near the defunct golf course designed by Donald Ross in 1926 and played often by Bobby Jones. The other site was closer, in fact, not far from my cottage and near the big head. The big head was a campus landmark set in a grass field. It was a six-foot tall bust of Franklin Delano Roosevelt, or FDR, sitting on a base, almost hovering in the air. It was unusual but appropriate, I suppose, as he had once owned the entire place.

Overall the RWS campus was several hundred acres, much of it now woods and fields, perched on a hill. It included the famous pools of warm water that FDR swam in, the abandoned golf course, abandoned dorms, and a few private residences, and quite a few abandoned cottages moldering in place all around campus and in the woods. The campus itself was surrounded on three sides by nearly ten thousand acres of state park. The largest park in the state.

Although in middle Georgia, the park centered on a mountain ridge long ago orphaned from the Appalachian range much further north. Pine Mountain ran nearly east-west for several miles and across parts of three counties. Creeks ran down the ridge among rocks forming small waterfalls. Totally different than most creeks in this area, which were usually slow moving and tepid seeps of orange mud. Pine Mountain also hosted a vestigial biome composed of Appalachian species, a few of which were mountain laurel and rhododendron.

The name of Pine Mountain was also confusing, as it referred to various geographical features besides the mountain ridge itself. The actual long ridge was called Pine Mountain across its length. But also near one end on the north side was Pine Mountain the town. Nearby was Pine Gardens the resort. Further east and on the south side of the ridge was a community called Pine Mountain Valley. It was nearly as confusing as the overuse of the word Peachtree in Atlanta.

Altogether, the mountain and its surroundings were a most unusual. I was here hiding from life, and the decaying RWS campus gave me a little island of quiet. Emma and I had always wanted to live on a college campus. Fulfilling that dream was left to me.

CHAPTER THREE

After breakfast I strolled around the quad. I don't know if anybody called it that other than me. But it seemed like one. In front of the Georgia Hall a road encircled a large area of grass and trees. Interspersed were large houses and cottages once a vital part of campus where people lived and worked. Most were built in the 1920s and 1930s. Much more recently a large, modern dormitory was added for students working toward a technical career. Walking around the circuit was nearly a half mile. My cottage, the house next door that was now the campus police station, and the chapel were across the road from that quad on one side. On the other side of the quad were other abandoned houses and the old dormitory now closed. Toward the back of the quad and across the road, was the big head and a large building that contained the fitness center. The rest of campus was behind the Georgia Hall, mainly the hospital and an office building for state employees. Those buildings also enclosed an area of grass and trees, composing the original quad.

Down the hill to the west behind the fitness center a road went to the old golf course. North of the quad, the hill sloped to the famous warm springs and the road to the town of Warm Springs. To the south of the quad was a large lake. Behind the lake was an extensive Boy Scout camp and retreat. It had not been used in a decade. Beside the lake was a loop road going uphill into the woods and onto the lowest shoulder of Pine Mountain. The other three private residences and a dozen abandoned cottages were set on large yards mostly grown with weeds. Just off that loop road was a back entrance into the Little White House.

Everything off the quad, away from the Georgia Hall, was filled with thick forest. Mostly pines and hardwoods with undergrowth of native wax myrtles, beauty berry bushes, hollies, young magnolias, and wild blueberries. A lot of the thickness was unfortunately due to the invasive species of Japanese privet and wisteria. Some of the wisteria vines were thicker than even the tree trunks. Eventually, the vines would strangle and bring down the trees. The wisteria seeds were large hard beans. In the fall, the substantial bean pods fell with the seeds and sounded like a hailstorm. No wonder the vines spread so easily. At least kudzu had not taken over the area. Cedar trees grew on the fringes of the woods where the light was better.

Ironically, the woods were not so thick from the

ground, up to about six feet. In many places, the underbrush was nearly clear except for the wisteria. I wondered how that happened. Did the campus pay the poor groundskeepers to clear the jungle? I figured it out quickly. The vast deer population ate everything they could reach. Ten thousand acres in middle Georgia free from hunting and little car traffic produced an abundance of deer. Browsing twelve hours a day, they ate their way through the jungle. Any given night I had a dozen of the insatiable browsers in my small yard.

My twenty-minute walk gave me two laps around the quad. Other than a few students walking to class and the grounds crew treating fire ant mounds, I saw no one, and no cars. Quite a change from how the place used to be according to stories I heard in the cafeteria and cursory research I had begun once moved in.

The campus had been an oasis for disabled people in a hostile world. An entire microcosm of diverse people ended up in a tiny place near a tiny town, at a time when they were not welcome most places. Apparently, FDR found a purpose in life besides politics and created a "colony" for those people. And for himself.

One thesis I found and read chronicled the early years of campus as researched by a graduate student twenty years ago. I wasn't sure how much was true, but apparently the place had a reputation for parties, gambling, and more intimate activities. Here the people shunned by society for being disabled had lived life hard and fun, perhaps making up for lost time and opportunity robbed from them by the polio virus.

People came from all over America. Wealthy scions of

New York, shopkeepers from St. Louis, and farmers from Mississippi. All looking for an escape from and cure for a crippling virus that cared not about age, sex, or social status. It was a safe space. It was also an innovative space funded by Franklin D. Roosevelt, the most famous resident. He was responsible for bringing in local people to help, plus therapists, doctors, and nurses. Along with the wealthy residents affected by polio came the poorer folks. FDR campaigned for funding to keep everything going, as well as investing much of his own money. Polio had no regard for socio-economic status, so FDR found innovative ways to pay for the less wealthy patients.

Pushers and physiotherapists were the young lifeblood of the campus operation. Pushers were the athletic and handsome local boys and young men. The physiotherapists were new graduates from a small college in Tennessee. Trained in nursing and therapy, they were selected for their work ethic, intelligence, and how they looked in a bathing suit. Doctors and specialists came to campus. Housing and a hospital were needed and built, bringing more workers. People were people, regardless of disability or status, so romances began and flared out, ending in heated arguments, marriage, or both.

Social life was nonstop as even the daily therapy was decidedly social. Days were spent at the pool where individual therapists worked with each patient, but it was in a group setting. Nights were spent the same way, as many of the same groups congregated at the designated cottage on campus for impromptu entertainment and the ever-present card games. Physiotherapist girls in their long dresses and hats, pusher boys in their pants and shirts, patients in evening attire as they tended to be wealthier. Parties went late and sometimes became raucous. In the middle of nowhere Georgia, a tiny egalitarian society existed. Of course, it couldn't last. Franklin D. Roosevelt, the driving force, died in 1945. He left money and land holdings for the RWS campus, but the early expansion fueled by his determination and charisma was gone. But the operations and campus continued.

The Salk polio vaccine was released in 1955. It did not get much traction at first but was introduced en masse by the early 1960's. Polio became an endangered virus in humans and rightly so. Along with the cure, the very purpose for the campus was now over. Existing patients were still on site, but new ones trickled in slowly, then not at all. Changes were made, and other illnesses and victims of accidents were treated at the hospital. But the heart of the campus slowed nearly to a stop. Early patients that became residents died or left, and the same fate befell all the early staff. The network of campus cottages fell into disrepair as they could not be sold to the public or lived in, as the state took over operations. Only a few of the cottages had been held privately, and by luck I found one the day it went up for sale.

Recently, a new wave of change had come, and students were now on campus, and the hospital was still active. There was still hope to save the campus, but age and disrepair were going to be tough to overcome. I thought about all that on the short quad walk. It was difficult not to think about it as I walked past historical vacant buildings with peeling paint, loose siding, and shrubs and vines growing into the porches. The campus needed attention to get funds, but that very attention would bring in a lot more people. And that would change the sleepy place where I had found my escape. The campus might not make it much longer without those funds, however. It was a good news, bad news situation. Disrepair was as much a result of being unknown and out of the way as anything, which also kept people away and the campus nice and quiet.

But enough facilities like the cafeteria and fitness center remained which made my life better. The little-used fitness center contained everything that the title implied, plus more. Add-ons included an Olympic pool, bowling alley, indoor track, and large craft room. It was worthy of a college campus or city. I could use it any time of the day or night and sometimes I would be there by myself. On a busy day there might be ten other people in the building. I spent time there on a stationary bike when the winter weather was rainy or when the blazing sun was out in summer.

On my return, Kat greeted me from her perch on the back of the sofa scooted up under a front window. She kept an eye on the birdfeeder from there. I scratched her a bit and she plopped her head back down. Already fed, she was into one of her thirty naps of the day. Kat had at least eight different meows. She employed them according to her needs which were more like demands. But she was politely demanding. She also trilled more than any cat I ever knew. She entered and exited a room with a trill and when she jumped up on a chair, the bed, or sofa, and again when she jumped down. When I touched her she trilled. Same when she rolled onto her back. Or when I walked to the refrigerator. I enjoyed the communication and had learned about slow blinks and nose-to-nose touching, so she trained me well.

I spent the rest of the day working a few minutes in the yard, then working around the exterior of the cottage. It needed excavating down to the foundation to access termite damage. I took a break to get groceries, then finished the cottage work. The evening was spent site-planning for the campus garden. The first thing was to find money to order fence posts, wire and an electric fence charger. Otherwise the deer would harvest whatever was grown. I did an evening walk and a little writing afterward. The life of a bored gentleman. At least outwardly.

CHAPTER FOUR

The next morning, I left my house on another walk. I intended to hike past the lake to connect to a path to a waterfall. The path climbed up Pine Mountain and was in the state park. Twice a week I took the route to break up just walking about campus. First order was to cross campus to the large man-made lake and pass by the old Boy Scout camp retreat. Instead of going through the camp, I walked on the flat grassy top of the extensive dam. On the other side of the lake, the route went through an old construction site where dead lawnmowers retired from the campus grounds were stored. After that it was all woods, creeks, and the official Pine Mountain trail up to the waterfalls. I enjoyed the change of scenery walking through the woods which reminded me of the mountains because of the rhododendrons and mountain laurel.

The long dam ended on the far side of the lake where a grass spillway was located for flood overflows. It was just a flat, shallow grassy spot, behind which the hill, really the back of the dam, fell off to a distant creek. I doubted the lake had ever overflowed. But the shallow slope allowed geese easy entry into the water, as well as Boy Scout canoes in the past. Grassed to almost the edge of the water, there was a small strip of bare soft dirt marking where the water level fluctuated. Just beyond the spillway grass and going along the rapidly steepening bank, large wax myrtles grew under the pines and overhung the water. A big wax myrtle was only a few feet from where I stood, stretching to nearly twenty feet since it was growing in nearly full sun. Fifty feet in front of the spillway was a small island with large pines and more wax myrtles. Perfect for the wood ducks and geese that frequented the lake.

I stopped to look at something odd that had not been here on my last hike. A small pile of clothes and a pair of shoes were on the grass near the water. Was someone swimming? It was prohibited but not unheard of for someone to grab a swim in the calm water. I turned to scan the lake but saw no one. I stood still and waited two minutes. Still, I saw no one, and I doubted anyone would be underwater that long. Well, anyone alive. A bad feeling flared up. Without moving, I took out my phone. I took pictures of everything around me. Including my footsteps clearly showing in the morning dew on the grass. I also took pictures of the lake, including the overgrown area to my right, past the spillway. Especially the large wax myrtles that came to the water's edge and overhung slightly.

I started looking at the lake pictures and zoomed in. Under the wax myrtles, more than fifty feet away, I saw something I could not quite make out. But it was eerie enough that I quit looking at the pictures and called Bryan, chief of the RWS campus police. Most recently we had chatted over coffee two days ago in the cafeteria. But as a next-door neighbor, he was one of the first people I had gotten acquainted with when I moved here. We got along well and talked several times a week about non-police business.

"Campus police, this is Edna."

"Hi Edna, is Bryan in? This is James Wilder."

"Yes, just a moment." I heard a click, silence, then Bryan picked up.

"Hi James."

"Hey Bryan."

"What can I do for you?"

"I might be bringing you some bad news. I'm standing on the spillway of the lake, on the far side. There are some clothes here on the bank, and I think there could be a body over under the wax myrtles. I can't see for sure and I don't want to go walking around and disturb anything."

"Oh no. Stay there, and please try not to walk around or pick anything up. I'll be there in three minutes." He hung up and I imagine he was rushing out to the car. Thirty seconds later, I saw his police SUV moving fast across campus, then onto the lake road. It made a wide loop up above the old camp through the trees and I could hear the car speeding. He didn't have lights or siren on, but he didn't need either since there were no cars or people about.

Meanwhile, I walked backwards away from the lake, stepping into my own footprints. I stopped about fifty feet away. Two minutes later Bryan's car came to an abrupt halt at the gate on the other side of the spillway, in the small parking area. He got out and made a wide semicircle away from the lake to come to where I stood. He knew his business better than most small-town police.

"Hi James."

"Hi Bryan."

"Before you say anything, I'm going to stand here and look for a minute. I need to get the scene in my head before doing anything further."

I nodded.

"OK, how long have you been here?" he asked a moment later. "And what have you seen?"

"I've been here about ten minutes. I was on the way to my waterfall hike. You can see my footprints in the dew along the dam behind us, then over near the clothes. I backtracked here in my own prints. The first thing I saw were the clothes. I stood a while watching the lake to see if anyone was swimming. After a few minutes of no swimmer in sight, I started scanning the water over under the bushes. From that distance I can't be sure, but I think there might be something under there. That is when I called you." I did not mention taking pictures.

"Good. If this is a crime scene the disturbance is minimal. I'm going to take some photos, then check the clothes. Stay put." He took out his phone and got photos of the scene and my footprints. Then he put on gloves and walked over to the clothes. He moved the shoes from the top of the piled clothes, checked the shirt for a second, then the pockets in the pants. From what I saw, there was nothing in the pockets. He walked back to me.

"James, if you would please walk over to my car. Try to stay in my footprints as much as possible. I'll be behind you. From the car I'll go to the bank and work through the wax myrtles while you stay at the car."

"Sure."

We did so, and I leaned on the car while he fought through the thick wax myrtle thicket. Five minutes later he was back. Sweaty yet looking pale.

"It is what you thought it was. I have to call this in since we don't have the full resources to process the scene. I hate to ruin your day, but can you stick around? I'll need a written statement which we can do back at the station. Once the state guys get here, I'm sure they will want to talk to you."

"I can do that." Not that I thought I had much choice. I was the first one at the scene so I understood.

"Good. Now I'm calling Edna to get a couple of guys out here to secure the scene. Then we can go to the office."

Ten minutes later we were at his office. From his window I could see the side of my house through the wisteria vines. I wrote down everything I had seen and done that morning at the lake. Except for taking the photos. Something was nagging my brain, and I knew the pictures might answer the nag. I also worried that Bryan or the state guys might confiscate my phone.

"Thanks James for putting that in writing," Bryan said.

"The state guys won't be here for a while so you can go home. We will walk over later."

"I thought a body would get them here a lot faster."

"Oh, state forensics and the coroner are already at the lake. The two investigators are what we are waiting for."

"Got it. I'll see you later."

Back in my kitchen I built a sandwich. I wasn't hungry much, but needed to occupy one level of my brain while I churned through some things. Something wasn't right, beyond the fact that there was a body in the lake. But I didn't know yet what was bothering me. I decided to make a list of what I knew. I also took time to transfer the photos to my computer and erase them from my phone. It seemed prudent to do that before talking to the state police. I also decided against studying the pictures before talking to the police.

I started my list of known observations. I had approached the lake on a quiet morning with no waves. Little to no wind as there was a heavy dew. There was a pile of clothes and a pair of shoes beside the lake. There was not much disturbance of the wet dirt between the grass and the edge of the water. A body was on the edge of the lake, under the wax myrtles, fifty feet or more from the pile of clothes. Possibly more like seventy feet. The night before had been a little chilly but calm. I had not seen a vehicle in the area. That was what I had observed in a general sense. Now I needed to think about details.

Based on the size of the shirt and pants I saw when Bryan picked them up, the deceased was likely a young person or female. I would probably find out soon enough, so I put that aside for now. The dew on the grass was not disturbed, so the person must have gone into the water last night or before then. A pair of pants and a shirt on the grass told me the person was not wearing underwear or socks, or they were still on the body. I also tabled that thought for later. No identification signified the person had none, or it had been removed. No vehicle, so the person had walked or had come with someone that drove away. Possibly with the identification. I wasn't sure I liked where the implications were taking me.

I put away the list to think. The simplest explanation was that someone young or female had gone for a midnight swim and drowned. The second most likely explanation was the person had walked into the lake on purpose without any intention of coming back. Another possibility, and least likely considering this was Warm Springs, was that a murder had been committed. I put the matter away in my mind and ate the sandwich on my front porch. There was a lot of activity next door. I imagine Bryan's life had gotten infinitely more complicated. He was a former police officer from a big city, so he had likely seen a dead body before. Through the trees and vines, I saw an unfamiliar dark sedan pull in. I was about to get busy myself.

CHAPTER FIVE

An hour later I saw Bryan with two others walk over to my drive. I waved as they approached. Both strangers had the typical police look. The man had dark hair, cut short, and a grey suit, no tie. The woman had auburn hair and a navy pantsuit.

"James, this is Agent Sims," he said, indicating the female. "And Agent Woods. State investigators from the Georgia Bureau of Investigation. You can imagine the topic of discussion."

I shook hands with both. "I'm sure I know the subject. Would you be more comfortable speaking here or next door?" I noticed Bryan had not told them my name as I was sure they already knew it.

"Next door would be better," Woods said.

"Sure, I'm ready."

A minute later we all sat down in Bryan's office.

"Mr. Wilder, we already have your written statement," Woods said. "But we would like you to tell us what happened this morning. Please be as detailed as possible."

I went through everything again. All I added was that there were no vehicles in the parking area near the spillway. I noticed Woods was asking the questions while Sims took notes. Some roles are just assumed I guess, even at the GBI. Man talks, woman notates.

"Thank you, Mr. Wilder," Woods said. "Or should I call you something else?"

"Mister is fine, I don't use Doctor anymore. James is also fine."

"I'll continue with Mr. Wilder. Where were you last night?"

I had expected the question. "If you will allow, I'll start with the afternoon. I did some yard work and digging out the foundation of my guest cottage. About 3 pm I was in Woodbury getting groceries. I was home by 4:30 and walked to the cafeteria on campus to get a salad. Afterwards I worked on my guest cottage in the backyard a bit, then did my usual walk around campus between 7 and 8. I wrote at home until about midnight, then went to bed."

"Thanks. Do you live alone?"

"Yes."

"Did anyone see you last evening?"

"Inside my house, no. I did a few texts, but otherwise I did not see or communicate with anyone. As for when I was outside, the folks in the cafeteria saw me when I went to get a meal. When I was walking the patrol car passed twice but you'd have to ask Bryan who was on duty."

"Thank you for answering. Why were you at the lake this morning?"

"It is part of my normal hiking route. Twice a week I cut across the lake dam to go through the old service area to hit the Pine Mountain trail up to the waterfalls. The rest of the week I stay on campus or go up to the Little White House to walk."

"I have one last question. From where you were standing by the lake, you said you saw the body."

"No, I did not."

"I can look at your statement or ask Bryan here, but I think you did."

"No, I did not. From where I stood I thought I saw something in the water over by the bank under the bushes. When I called Bryan, I said the same thing. What I saw from that distance was indistinct, but based on the clothes and shoes, and no one about swimming, it made me think the worst and call Bryan. I told him there might be a body."

"OK, then, I understand. Thank you for your time. We will be in touch if we have more questions."

I shook hands again and left. It had gone just the way I expected. Now it was over I could get back to figuring out why the whole thing made me so unsettled. The easiest way to accomplish that was physical labor. And I had the perfect job for that.

The guest cottage behind my house was slightly younger than the main house, just under a hundred years. I assume it was built for either a servant or for out-of-state guests.

The floor of the guest cottage was more rotten than a pile of month-old dumpstered Dollar General produce. I expected some termite damage since every structure in the state over fifty years old had damage. But this was extensive. Luckily, it was only in one area of the kitchen. The little buggers had eaten a few floor joists, then the pine plank floor itself, then continued up into the wooden island that separated the kitchen and living areas. The only thing intact was the ancient formica top on the island. All the wood beneath it, in fact the entire island frame crumbled into dust when I tried to pry it loose where it was attached to the wall and floor. That's when I noticed the floor was just as eaten. I lightly stepped on it and my foot went through the floor and I saw the clay beneath.

I stopped for a moment while assessing the damage. Everything under the island was powder. About three feet by five feet was a total loss as far as flooring and joists. I guess I would not be refinishing the old plank floors unless I could find something similar to replace what was now gone. I used the shovel to knock out all the loose dusty remnants, then went outside and brought in the wheelbarrow. Stepping down onto the bare dirt beneath the floor, I began scooping up all the detritus that had fallen. There was also leaves and grass under the spot so other four-legged critters must have been under the cottage as well. A great big pest fest.

It took three loads to clear everything. Once all the junk was gone I took a saw and cut more floor and joists away from the damaged area to give it a clean edge. One joist stub had a termite trail leading to a main beam under a load-bearing wall that separated the cottage into two equal spaces. That could be bad or could be nothing. But it could wait for another day. Dropping back to the dirt I shoveled out all the stuff I had just cut free from the floor above.

There was a distinct chink when my shovel hit something. I was not surprised. A ninety-eight-year-old building was bound to have some pieces of metal, broken glass, or busted ceramics underneath it. Whatever it was lay partially buried in the dry clay. Ah, an old whiskey bottle buried during Prohibition, maybe. I bent down to work on it with my gloved hands to keep from breaking it. A minute later I had it out and was surprised it was an intact glass bottle. Not a whisky or wine bottle, however. It looked more like a medicine bottle, perhaps a quart in size, made of thick clear glass and sealed with a heavy glass stopper. But it was so dusty I could not see if anything was inside. I set it aside while I finished cleaning up the floor remnants.

I took the bottle back to the house and wiped it off, then set it on a shelf. I would wait before opening it as I had plenty of other things to do. Foremost was studying the photos I had taken this morning. But after I took a shower.

First, I transferred the photos from the computer downloads folder and put them on a spare external hard drive and erased them from the computer. It would not get past a real computer hacker, but for the amateur searcher, such as the local or state police, I was probably safe. I doubted it was illegal, but it seemed unwise to photograph a crime scene taken before the police had been called. Having them on the computer and off my phone made me feel better, plus gave me more options to study each photo, or just a portion of it. I could zoom in or out as necessary.

Looking through the photos, I began cataloging my misgivings from earlier. Something was amiss. I hoped Bryan, or whoever ended up in charge of the investigation was good at what they did.

I zoomed in on photos taken of the bank under the wax myrtles. With enough magnification, a body was visible. The head was too close to the bank to make out anything like a face or hair, and they were face down in the water. It was blurry, but I could make out a bra and panties but no socks. The deceased was female.

The longer I studied the pictures, the more discrepancies I saw. Whatever the story was, I felt the person had not voluntarily walked into the lake, and someone else was involved. I based that on what I'd observed in person and after viewing the pictures.

First, I did not know anyone that, as they undressed, put their clothes on the ground and then shoes on top. If I took off my clothes by the lake, shoes would come off first. Then clothes, and they would be laid on top. At least that would be the order in my world. I thought back, then checked the pictures. Shirt on bottom, then pants, then shoes. No socks with the clothes and none on the body.

Second, there were no clear footprints under the water leading from the pile of clothes to deeper water. There were a couple of larger odd impressions out in the water, but nothing resembling footprints showing she waded in. She could have walked somewhere else to enter the water, but nobody in Georgia went around barefoot anymore because of fire ants. Plus, snakes were already out with the warm weather. There was one impression with a pattern embedded in the mud between the grass and water. Whatever it was, it did not look like a footprint. The type of shoe found with the clothes did not have that type of tread either. The pattern was oddly familiar, but I could not place it.

Where and how did she get in the lake? She didn't walk in, and the water was only a foot deep even three feet from shore, so she didn't jump or dive in. Which way was the wind blowing that night? I checked the weather for last night. Yes, a light breeze was blowing, and it would have pushed her back against the lakeshore from where she went in the water. And that brought up the question of why was she floating after so short a time in the water?

I had convinced myself somebody put her in the water. If she was conscious, I doubt she would have gone in voluntarily. I would need to get the coroner's report to see if they had found any evidence she had been strangled or knocked out. What else would be on the list? Drugs, alcohol, gas, car exhaust? I needed the report, but I doubted anyone was going to offer it to me. I rarely let legal logistics get in the way when something important needed to get done, however. But I would try another way before doing anything illegal.

Late in the evening I walked around campus to fend off the bad two hours. From a distance I saw two jonboats on the lake. Probably police checking for more evidence. I doubted they would find anything.

I went back to study the photos again. Kat watched me but gave no help. In fact, she occupied one of my hands for her last belly rub of the evening. I gave up on the photos and Kat and I retired for the night. Or tried to. My brain kept going back to why the body was floating.

Based on my premise, she had gone missing on Wednesday night, so she went into the water after dark. With the water temperature being slightly warm, if she drowned she would have sunk and not floated up for a couple of days. Yet she was floating within a few hours, which indicated no water in the lungs. Sort of a declaration that she didn't drown unless there were other factors I didn't know about.

CHAPTER SIX

"Good morning George," I said.

"Hi James. Hungry this Friday morning?"

"Partially. Trying to decide whether to jumpstart my day with caffeine or carbs."

"I would recommend both."

"I like the way you think."

"Guess that means pancakes along with eggs, bacon, and coffee?"

"A great start. I've got a pile of cottage remodel detritus to move today so I'll work off the meal."

George grabbed my order and I paid out a grand total of five dollars at the register. My plate in hand I headed for the coffee canister. My cup full, I carefully walked to a nearby table with a familiar face.

"Hi Ison."

"Hello James. I see you are keeping to your schedule. Probably best since you've had an exciting day or two."

"You've already heard."

"Oh yes, the campus telegraph has been working overtime."

"Telegraph would be appropriate for this campus. Maybe online social media will visit sometime in the future. Mess everything up."

"It's already here. My email was full this morning and you are a topic of conversation on the 'I Love Warm Springs' social media site."

"Great, just what I wanted."

"It's not so bad. Only about 30% think you did it."

"What?"

"The murder. After a torrid affair full of sado-masochistic acts and possibly Satanic group sex."

"You are kidding, right? Nobody even knows who it is or how it happened."

"Mostly kidding. But in this small town, people's imaginations do run amok. It's a terrible tragedy, but people need a story. Making one up is nearly as good as the real thing. Sometimes better."

"The information vacuum gets filled with nonsensical ten-second videos from teenage influencers."

"Pretty much."

"Thanks for telling me I guess."

"Bringing joy is what I do."

I looked up to see Ison's colleague walk in and giving me a sour face. "Why is Old Cranky looking so sour this morning?" It was what I called the man that never said hello to me or anyone else, especially the cafeteria workers when he came in. Which was odd since he worked in the building. His name was Benjamin Rawley, not that he had ever introduced himself. "Might be the only time he has ever actually noticed me."

"Benjamin is upset about the situation. Not about the unfortunate person's death, but because the deceased had the bad taste to expire on campus and make his life slightly more difficult."

"Oh, one of those types."

"Lack of empathy is one of his many faults. Along with assigning blame. Hopefully you won't have to experience the multitude of others."

We finished eating and I excused myself. I had plenty of work to do, plus I wanted to get away from the public eye. I had more demolition to do pulling sheetrock off the walls of the bedroom. My hope was that the pine plank walls in other parts of the cottage were under the old drywall. Manual labor gave me more time to consider a couple of things on my mind. By lunchtime I was tired and dirty. I rinsed off, changed, and walked down to the cafeteria for a salad. My plan, as usual, was to spend tomorrow cooking, as Saturday was cook day. No reason then, to spend the effort today.

As I walked past the police station next door, I noticed more cars than usual. Odd for a Friday afternoon, but I knew this was one of the most unusual weeks on campus for years. I packed up my salad in the takeout box in the cafeteria and walked back. Bryan was outside the police station talking to two others. I had a hard time calling it that rather than the police house, because it truly was a campus house with police inside. He saw me and walked up to the road while the other two went in.

"Hey Bryan."

"Hi James."

I noticed we were talking outside. Away from his official post and not at my house. In public view but out of earshot of anyone. It could be a coincidence, but I thought not.

"I'm betting you are staying busy these days."

"More so than I'd ever dreamed of in this sleepy town."

"Sorry about that."

"Yeah, but it's not your fault. You know how these things work. Active investigation and all, so I can't say much. But anything the public already knows is fair game."

"Thanks. I guess I'm curious like a lot of people, but I'm hesitant to ask you about the investigation."

"I appreciate it. There is a tentative press conference scheduled for later. I have to go. The state guys, county sheriff, and coroner will be there and a statement will be released."

"All the usual suspects in attendance."

"Strength in numbers."

"What is that going to tell us, or is it a secret until then?"

"Nothing is a secret around this town. We have identified the body. Other than a few other details that is about it. They are trying to decide whether to announce a probable cause of death. Right now they are leaning toward accidental drowning."

"Who was it?"

"Her name was Tammy Wilkins. A realtor and mom

from near the town of Pine Mountain. Although she had a Hamilton address."

"Name sounds slightly familiar. Probably from my time last year looking at listings."

"Since you were searching down here you probably did see her name. One of the bigger, or at least older firms around here."

"Any idea what she was doing in Warm Springs?"

"Not yet. She went to a church function Wednesday evening, then her husband said she never came home. He called the county sheriff in the middle of the night. I doubt they made much of an effort and didn't bother to alert us. Probably sitting in their office in Hamilton and drinking coffee."

"There was not a car by the lake. It's a long walk from Pine Mountain. Ten miles?"

"The car was found at the visitors' parking lot down the hill in front of campus. Her ID was in her purse in the passenger seat."

"Even from there it is quite a walk to the lake at night. That lot is dark, especially toward the back. There also are not any cameras near that lot, are there?"

"No cameras. It is quite dark under the trees."

"Was the car pulled in or backed in?"

"Backed in. Why, does that matter?"

"I don't think so. Just curious about her habits."

"It did throw us off for a day. County sheriff and the state police were looking for it, but it was a common SUV. Because it was backed in, nobody bothered to check the tag for a while."

"Did her socks ever turn up?"

"Her socks? What do you mean?" Bryan was giving me a calculating look.

"I saw the pile of clothes myself, and I was there when you picked them up. I did not see any socks."

"Her socks, or a pair of worn socks, were in the car, thrown in the backseat."

"Just curious if the car was dusted for fingerprints."

"Ordinarily I wouldn't tell you, but in this case, it doesn't matter, since none were found."

"You mean only her prints were found in the car."

"No, none at all."

"Then it might be possible someone used her socks to wipe down the car after they left it there."

"I cannot say that officially. And please don't say anything either. You seem to have something on your mind. Want to share it?"

"I have thoughts. But I don't want to interfere with an ongoing investigation. Last thing I want to do is influence the investigators away from the truth if I'm wrong."

"Glad you don't want to interfere. But?"

"But it was not an accidental drowning."

"That is something you don't want to say out loud right now. I think I understand where you are coming from, but those in charge are leaning away from a wrongful death."

"Despite what the evidence says."

"I can't get into that. Tammy was a well-known, and liked, person in the Pine Mountain and Hamilton communities. A suicide ruling is not going to help her husband or kids. Saying murder out loud would light a powder keg. At least accidental drowning is slightly better."

"I was not talking about suicide either. That leaves only one option."

"I know. But there were no signs at all of any kind of violence. The majority consensus is, well, I've already said it."

"I know. I understand the logic of coming to that conclusion. But it is wrong."

"You don't hold back, do you? Do you know something we don't?"

"First, I have less information than the investigators. I just look at it differently. But I'm an outsider to the investigation, obviously. I'm also a newcomer to the community, which means an outsider in the larger sense. Nobody is going to care what I think. I'll let things happen as they may, for now."

"Then what? I'm not asking as Chief, but as a citizen, somebody interested in that justice is done if appropriate."

"I don't know. But if she was murdered, I'll do what I have to. I'm not being a vigilante or anything, but I'd put a case forward once I have one."

"Why? You didn't even know her."

"Doesn't matter. Happened on my watch, in a way. The community is too small to support a murderer."

"Just don't do anything rash. At least talk to me or the state investigators. And my office requires me to tell you to stay out of it."

"We both know I have selective hearing."

"Yeah. I know. Have a good weekend."

"You too, Bryan." My unofficial interview was over. I hoped I had put enough doubt in his mind that he would re-look at the evidence. He was smart enough to know that the car being wiped down was enough to doubt an accidental drowning, but he could not say it.

I continued the arduous journey of another hundred feet to my house. My next errand was to examine the bottle from the guest cottage.

I picked it up and began working on removing the glass stopper. It stubbornly remained shut. Eventually, I put it under warm water to clean it better and see if the heat would help to loosen the stopper. As the dirt washed away, I noticed what looked like paper rolled up inside, and finally the stopper loosened. I dried it off and popped the stopper. Looking inside, there were definitely a few pages of paper with elegant but faded writing. I could not gently shake them out as the old papers were rolled up. Must have been how they were placed in the bottle, but now they had partially unrolled and were wider than the narrow bottle top. I found my forceps from a former career and teased out the pages without any major damage inflicted.

Carefully unrolling the paper and placing a weight on the corners, I saw the handwriting was indeed elegant. I picked up the first page and saw writing on the back. Same for the other two pages. The ink was so faded that perhaps one of every ten words was clearly legible. Another twenty percent of the words I could decipher with a magnifier and close lighting. The other seventy percent or so was lost to my eyesight. I saw a few names, and they repeated enough that I got three full names. Other names were partial first or last names, or maybe place names. The only other fact was that it was dated, or at least referenced, 1945. The papers could have been in the bottle for more than eighty years.

I opened my laptop and searched for the names. I expected one or more of them to be a former owner of the house and guest cottage. My other thought was they would be associated with the campus or town. But I only found one of the names, and it was in reference to a tragic death in Warm Springs. I printed off that brief article. I needed to think about what to do next. But I knew I needed to do a deep dive into the history of this place to find out anything further. Then I had an epiphany.

It was Friday afternoon, so it was probably futile, but I called a former colleague from the University of Georgia. One of my former careers was working with multi- and hyperspectral imaging of surfaces. The cameras could pick up wavelengths invisible to humans. Paper was a little out of the scope of what the lab typically studied. Yet if anyone could make out the faded writing in a short time it would be them.

Surprisingly, Albert picked up on the third ring.

"Albert, this is James. How are you?"

"Well this is a surprise. Thought you were out of the country."

"Came back four years ago. Was in Asheville but now in Warm Springs."

"Oh my, that tiny place? Can't be for work."

"No, more of an early retirement escape."

"How is Emma? Didn't see her as a small-town girl."

"She died last year."

"James, I'm so sorry. I didn't know."

"It's alright Albert. I have not told anyone outside of the immediate family, really." I pushed on to get past the awkward moment. "Albert, are you still running imaging research?"

"Yes, we are. Is this a work call?"

"Sort of. I found an interesting manuscript but can't read all of it. It is intact, but the ink is faded."

"Not our usual thing. But it should not be a problem for us to decipher it. Is it an important document?"

"Not sure. It could be something good or just a diary entry from 1945."

"I have a student working this semester, but I don't have enough work to keep him busy. I'll have him take a look and do a full analysis. It will be good training for him on the cameras and algorithm writing before we get into the real research project this fall."

"Thank you for looking at it."

"Sure. Are you sending it or bringing it over?"

I thought a moment. I had not been to Athens in a while. "I'll bring it up in a week or two. Give me a chance to see the place again."

"Give me a call the day you come up."

"I will. Thanks again Albert."

CHAPTER SEVEN

I t did not always work out, but I tried to leave a large block of time open on Saturday for preparing and cooking food. I made forays to the cafeteria during the week and Mable's on the weekend for breakfast. Sometimes back to the cafeteria for a salad, but otherwise I tried to prepare my own food. Not that what I made was always great, but because I knew too much about what happened in the commercial food world. I had lists of things to never buy or consume.

That left me to make my own. I enjoyed cooking as long as I wasn't rushed for time or trying to impress. Cooking food was one of the few areas in life where I could combine art and science and make it what I wanted it to be.

Many years ago, on a trip to Italy I learned that simple almost always equals better. Four or five ingredients, if fresh and good quality, could be made into something better than any of the menu items in an Italian restaurant in America. It was not a concept reserved for Italy, it applied to foods from all regions of the world. In that sense, more was usually not better. More has been added to cover up poor quality ingredients or for monetary reasons.

But first was my weekly brunch at Mable's Diner in Warm Springs. It was about a mile walk, so the two-mile trek would help work off the food. It was not effective because I used the walk as an excuse to get an extra pastry. The first half mile was on campus and nothing but thick forest. At the bottom of the hill I turned right onto the sidewalk along the road going into town. A few cars and a logging truck were the only traffic. Minutes later I was downtown.

Warm Springs was a mostly cute town central to nowhere. In a triangle between Columbus, Macon, and Lagrange, it was forty minutes to an hour or more to any of those cities. The cotton mill in Manchester once provided steady employment for the residents but it had closed long ago. Most people now commuted to jobs in the larger towns.

The area was known for tree farms, deer hunting compounds, and hobby farms for wealthy Atlantans. Lately there was a small influx of professional baseball players buying land for hunting plantations. Overall it was rural Georgia, with lots of trees, thick undergrowth and slow-moving muddy streams. And it was cut through by a high ridge that made no sense geologically. Warm Springs sat at the base of the odd mountain, known as Pine Mountain.

Physically it was a one-stoplight town, with two small gas stations, a short row of buildings on either side of the major street through town, Broad Street. There was a Main Street, but ironically it was a back lane. The short row of old brick buildings was about what any small southern town had. A few offices, restaurant, and retail shops catering to Atlanta tourists. Luckily one of the old store-fronts had Mable's Diner. It sounded old but was fairly new to town. A couple opened it as a coffee shop serving sandwiches for lunch, but it had morphed into a Southern-fusion diner. Which worked well with both locals and tourists. I went because they served my favorite coffee from an Athens roaster.

The town used to be a passenger train stop, bringing people to the healing springs. But the depot had not been functional in many years. The railroads still ran but freight only, with no commuter service. The depot did not even have an active rail link anymore. The town did have a federal fish hatchery that was over a hundred years old. Ironically it was on the other side of town from the warm springs, and had been built there because there was a large cold spring good for rearing fish.

I opened the door to the diner to see it mostly full. I sat at the counter as I didn't want to occupy a table for four.

"Cat dragged you in for another Saturday, huh?" asked Lottie.

"Yep, I'm dragged in like a chewed rat. Is that the special today?"

"I'll go get one and make it special for you." She left my coffee and went to handle another order.

Lottie was older, snappy, and irrepressible. Some might call her crusty, but I doubted they would live seconds past saying it out loud in her presence. She did not suffer fools or old men like me. Possibly because there was little difference. She called me old, but I was probably twenty-five years younger than she was. Lottie knew everything, everyone, and everything about everyone in town but rarely passed it on.

"I checked on the rat but we're out. Whattaya have?" she said as she came back.

"Southern omelet and fruit cup, please."

"Be out in a few. More coffee?"

"Yes, thanks."

She brought my food minutes later. The omelet was whatever was fresh in the garden at the moment per chef's choice. Could be any of the greens, onion, tomato, squash, okra, or peppers. Basically, anything but peas or beans. The cook would also add some bacon, sausage, or country ham, depending on what was in the kitchen. The surprise was part of the fun of ordering it. The fruit was usually heavy on blueberries since they grew abundantly in the area. I polished it off and kept an eye on the pastry case. I didn't walk as much this week as I normally did, so I considered passing.

"You keep eyeing them dainties and you're going to have to ask them out."

"Problem is I'm afraid one would say yes."

"Don't get your hopes up. The eclairs have too much class."

I decided to let that line of conversation fade before I said something stupid.

"Quiet all of a sudden?" Lottie asked. "Smart. Say, the resident talkers are yakking that you found that girl on the news."

"Yeah, I did. Ruined my hike. But I'm sure her day was a lot worse."

"I expect so."

"Did you know her?"

"Indirectly." Once Lottie got to one-word answers, it meant she was through talking about the present subject. Or talking in code.

"It is a shame it happened."

"It is."

"I guess it will be all the news for the next month."

"I doubt it. They'll call it an accident and it will go away."

"That would be a shame." I followed that with a blank look. She squinted at that, then crossed her arms and leaned over the counter across from me. She shifted her eyes to either side to check if anyone was close enough to listen.

"We might be thinking the same thing," she said. "If so, we might need a conversation one of these days."

"I appreciate that. Meanwhile I'll keep coming for food. If there's more than just food on the menu, I'll definitely be interested."

"It's a small town. There is always more." She pulled back and went off to give a ticket to a customer.

Huh, that was a clear signal something was rolling around under the dark underbelly of Warm Springs.

Which was funny because I was pretty sure the town did not have an underbelly. If it did, it probably wasn't dark. I paid and walked home.

It was time to begin my food prep and cooking. My goal was to have fresh fruit, vegetables, and some cooked lean meat on hand each week. Kept me busy on Saturday and gave me a healthier food selection that was easy to grab and eat. Otherwise, I tended to skip meals, then overindulge when ravenous on whatever was closest to my hands and face. For example, fast food in Manchester. This process was how I disciplined my poor eating habits.

I chopped up several apples and pears. Those were tossed in a thick paste I made from lemon and finely powdered sugar. It coated the fruit pieces and kept them from turning brown for five days. I segmented a couple of oranges and added them to the mix. Easy substitutes were tangerines or a grapefruit, whatever was available. All the fruit went into a sealed bag which I put in the refrigerator. When I ate it, I usually cut up and added a banana. I had not yet found a foolproof way to keep the cut banana from turning brown for five days.

For fresh guacamole I pulled the skins off of six avocados and pulled out the seeds. I mashed them up and added a healthy dose of lime juice. It kept the guacamole from turning brown prematurely. I added a small amount of finely minced garlic and shallot plus a few spices. More mashing then I spooned it into a quart plastic bag. I pushed out any air, sealed it and placed it in the refrigerator. Removing excess air also helped prevent it from browning. I snipped off a bottom corner of the bag and squeezed out what I needed each day.

I had two heads of lettuce. The process of making a wedge salad was highly complicated. I pulled the core out, discarded the exterior leaves since that was where most bacterial and chemical contamination resided, and cut each head into four sections. Dropped them in a plastic bag and that was it. One of the simplest preps ever. I could pull a section out, add a few things plus olive oil and vinegar and have a great salad.

Recently I had a few adventures making bread, but results were mixed for the amount of time and effort required. Besides, I could get decent bread at Mable's. I had also tried simple cheese-making but stopped because it was an inefficient use of time. My breadmaking endeavor would likely succumb to the same fate.

I rarely cooked or ate red meat any longer. My standards were too high for the quality available. One of the problems was so many commercial operations used antibacterial sprays, especially peracetic acid. It was a fancy term for a commercial mix of vinegar and hydrogen peroxide. Most people had vinegar in their pantry and peroxide in their medicine cabinet. Mix them and you had a cheap antibacterial rinse. It was effective on most surfaces. Unfortunately, meat was not a surface that made for successful treatment despite the claims. It reduced the loosely attached bacteria, but did little for cells stuck on the surface. Worse, the nature of the rinse created compounds that produced off-odors and flavors, mostly through rapid oxidative rancidity. In short, it broke down the fat and made it stink. I could not even cook hamburger inside due to the smell.

Once or twice a year I did prepare and cook beef

brisket to make pastrami or pork shoulders to make North Carolina eastern-style barbecue. I could throw those in the freezer after cooking and have small portions as needed.

Most Saturdays I prepped and cooked a couple of chickens, or parts equal to that. I normally ate only the breast meat, but Kat enjoyed dark meat. It was a match made in poultry heaven.

I did not do anything fancy. Roast chicken was again about doing things simply, with a few ingredients and herbs. But occasionally I splurged and cooked up a French meat guinea. Yes, those weird birds found in some farm yards that made an awful racket when disturbed. But not exactly, as there was a commercial variety that was grown as they had more meat. Difficult to find on grocery shelves, I had a source in North Carolina and bought a case to put in the freezer. Thawed and cooked correctly, it looked like a chicken, but the flavor and texture were much better. The breast looked dark like a duck when raw but cooked up white. And the meat had an intrinsic flavor, as if it had been marinated with light herbs and citrus. An excellent experience.

Today was fruit, lettuce wedges, a few fresh vegetables, and two roasted chickens. Fresh, light, and healthy. I was feeling good about that until I remembered recent events.

I didn't agree with the investigation and I was going to get involved. I should not since I wanted to live a quiet life with no notice or controversy. Yet I needed to ensure the correct conclusions were made. Every other time this had happened, things got complicated and people got irritated. It might be necessary to do so again in this case.

CHAPTER EIGHT

Although delayed a few days, I finally made my twice-a-week walk up the trail to the waterfalls. The path leading from campus along the old road was mostly flat. Only one portion was a problem, as the old logging road on the far side of campus, past the lawnmower graveyard, was perennially wet. An old spring seep leaked water onto the road, and deep ruts held the water for a hundred yards. The only choice was to slog through three inches of water and mud or go off-road and walk on the edge of the woods. It was a bit rough and in the warmer seasons it was a risk to pick up a couple of ticks. But without waterproof boots it was necessary.

After leaving the muddy road there was also the necessity of jumping a creek because the Pine Mountain trail was on the other side. To get across I had tried various logs, rocks and even an old concrete dam that spanned the creek, but there were no sure bets on getting to the other side unscathed. Between the mud and the creek, I always wore comfortable, waterproof boots.

I crossed the creek without incident and started along the trail. It was mostly flat at first as it stayed along the creek. This section of trail had a loose thicket of wax myrtles. These were thinner and rangier than the larger, thicker ones at the lakeside because of the lack of direct sun. Depending on where they were grown and managed, they could be a shrub, a small tree, or a hedge. I preferred the natural form versus the hedge look. I stopped to look and check for berries. Small glossy evergreen leaves sprouted from sometimes twisted grey bark limbs. The leaves had a nice smell and the berries were famously known as bayberry. Native Americans used the plant for many purposes. Colonists learned from them to boil the berries to make candles with a pleasant scent. Now the scent was widely used in many products. The berries ripened in the fall and warblers flocked in to devour them. Now that spring was underway I hoped to catch a few later berries. but the birds had long since picked them clean. Overall, it was one of my favorite shrubs, a quintessential southern plant, just as much as a magnolia tree.

Across the creek I turned left onto the trail and began ascending one of the shoulders of Pine Mountain. The trail soon brought me to large thickets of rhododendron and mountain laurel. Although a slightly different variety, the size of the individual shrubs and the size of the thickets rivaled anything found in the Smoky Mountains. They dwelt beneath stands of oaks dwarfed by the poor soil and heat of summer. The stunted hardwoods reminded me of the trees found in the Boston Mountains of Arkansas. Interspersed with the oaks and other hardwoods were the great longleaf pines of South Georgia.

The trail went past a massive example of that species, with its name on a plaque. Big Ferney towered above anything nearby including the poplars. I doubted a pine this big existed anywhere outside of areas forbidden for logging. The land opened out into a cove full of big trees with primitive camping allowed underneath.

The pines and hardwoods kept things shady, and the further along the trail as it ascended Pine Mountain, the more it looked like mountain terrain. I kept going, and the trail crossed over the creek via a bridge and began another ascension, this one rather steep climbing a rocky ridge.

The slopes ascending Pine Mountain were a surreal landscape of mixed flora. This was one of my favorite sections of the trail. Walking up high on a shoulder of the ridge, the view was of an ocean of mountain laurel and rhododendron along the creek gorge, then the flat cove spot with even a glimpse of Big Ferney sticking up above the other trees. I stopped for a few minutes to enjoy the quiet away from other humans. In the off season, there might be two or three other people or pairs on the trail, with quite a few more in the summer. Today the traffic had been very light. One young couple and a dad with his girl scout-age daughter.

After sitting on my rock ledge, I continued up the ridge. The trail went back close to the creek and a few small waterfalls. Then on to the main attraction, Cascade Falls.

They weren't that big, but larger than most natural falls in the area. I stopped to admire them and to let another hiker already there get a head start along the trail in front of me. I continued uphill, eventually cresting the ridge everybody knew as Pine Mountain. There was a parking lot for the trail just off the road that traversed the length of the ridge. A large communication tower of some type shared the parking lot. The trail continued along the ridgeline paralleling the road. I usually didn't walk that section as I didn't like the road noise. But I needed the extra mileage as I'd missed a couple of walks with all the excitement lately.

Not far down the trail, I noticed orange markers of survey tape. I knew there were several private parcels scattered within the state park boundaries, as Roosevelt had not bought every single land lot. As I walked, I realized this was one of the bigger parcels. I wondered if it was surveyed for sale, for a conservation easement, or for road construction, so I decided to look up the owner on the county website when I got back. I could also ask around town if anyone knew what was going on. It was a beautiful piece of land with long-range views, and the ridgeline was known as a delicate ecosystem sensitive to any major development. It would be a shame to lose it to a subdivision or a set of condos.

The walk back was long but uneventful. And mostly downhill. That meant easier for most people, but not for me. My knees were shot from the age of sixteen due to sports injuries. No anterior cruciate ligaments or cartilage was catching up to me after a lot of years of walking. The stress of going downhill resulted in some swelling in both knees but I felt the walks were worth it. I just had to refrain from doing anything stupid like falling or trying to run downhill. If a black bear ever chased me I'd be an easy dinner. Not that my bad knees made a difference, because in the mountains I'd seen how fast they ran downhill.

On my way back from the Pine Mountain trail hike, I took the outer campus loop which took me by Millard's house. I often stopped by when I saw him out, which was about half the time. I figured one of us needed the conversation. If it was too hot or cold, or too late in the evening he was inside. But today he was on the porch, so I waved and stopped. His waistcoat of the day was an emerald green satin, with paisley designs of pink, purple, and orange.

"Come on up foreigner," he said. I probably would be one for another fifty years. You were not a native small-towner unless you were a third-generation resident.

"Afternoon, Millard. Looking good today."

"Hogwash. I look good every day."

"That you do. Much happening in Millardville?"

"Saw a big truck over by the lake the other night."

"Not surprised, the police SUV goes over sometimes."

"But this was on Wednesday evening." That got my attention.

"Really? That is a long way. I can barely even see the water from here." I could see sun glinting off the water through the trees but little else.

"Of course you can't see anything from here. Are you sure you can operate a lawn mower? I would not want to be responsible for a slow one like you cutting off their foot on my property. Come over to the side porch."

He got up and I followed him to where the covered

porch wrapped around the side of the house. Sitting there was a Schmidt-Cassegrain twelve-inch telescope. I had used one before. It was powerful enough to count hairs on a possum at a thousand yards. Not that I had ever done that. But I had been able to get a detailed look at Saturn's rings and a lot of nebula at night.

"I got it years back when I was into astronomy," he said. "Now it is too heavy for me to move off the porch to see the night sky. Since then, the views are much more terrestrial. Here, take a look."

He had a big two-inch eyepiece on the squat cylinder. The view through the trees was limited, but I could see the far side of the lake and a small slice of the grass spillway. Actually, once I got it into fine focus, I could see individual leaves of grass, which was incredible at that distance. Unfortunately, most of the spillway view was blocked. Part of the area to the left that included the paved parking area was visible.

"I noticed a truck going around the lake behind the old camp with its lights off. Stopped there at the lot where the gate bars vehicles from getting on the spillway. Could have been silver but the lighting was tricky. It was a light color paint, though. Couldn't see what was happening with all the trees. But it was the same night that woman went missing that you found."

"You sure it was a truck and not an SUV?"

"I'm old, not blind. I can tell the difference between something with a long bed and those fancy wagons."

"About how long did the truck stay?"

"Five or ten minutes. Only one way in or out, so when it started to come back around it gave me time to swing

Martha over a little as it went out. I got a good glimpse of the side of it. That's how I know it was a truck."

"Thanks for telling me, Millard. Did you notice anything else?"

"Nope, too much blockage. Could not even see into the cab, so maybe it had those shaded windows. Then again, it was night."

"That helps with filling in a missing piece. Are you going to tell the police?"

"Nah, they probably wouldn't take me seriously. Probably would not even come and see what Martha could do."

"If I go forward with this and some other stuff, they might want to talk to you."

"That's fine. But I'm not going to tell them first."

Millard's sighting of the truck was helpful in the sense that Tammy didn't get there by herself by walking from her car. The problem was that fifty percent of the local population drove trucks like the one Millard described. So, it did not get me closer to who did it. But I began to wonder what happened to her in that truck. Maybe she met someone in the front parking lot and they went to their rendezvous at the lake. Then something went bad, and she was put into the lake. Yet there were no marks on her body indicating anything physical happened to her. Which again brought me back to how she was killed.

I thought about it as I walked home, but I came up with nothing more than I already had. Figuring out a murder without all the clues was really annoying.

CHAPTER NINE

From Millard's house to mine was only a ten-minute walk. I spent the time thinking about our first meeting. He was one the first people that lived on campus that I met after I moved in. I did not know it at the time, but Millard Masden was a local legend that no one remembered any longer. I met him when I was out walking. He owned one of the other few private cottages on campus. He was one of those characters that makes small towns interesting. Especially since I didn't have cable.

Over time I learned Millard had grown up on campus as his parents were doctors at the hospital. He left town to go to college at Harvard because he was smart and had lots of good recommendations. He thought about going to medical school but ended up going into the sciences instead. At some point he spent time in graduate school at the University of Leiden to conduct research. Once he had been mayor of Warm Springs. He had also been in charge of the Warm Springs Institute on campus for the state of Georgia for a while. He seemed to have success regardless of the area he was working in at the time.

Some of that I found during our talks, and some when I looked him up. He was quite accomplished and now lived as a semi-hermit on the other side of campus. It reminded me that a lot of old people, one of which I was rapidly becoming, that bore a notable past that no one knew about. How much knowledge was out there, unknown and untapped, and slowly ebbing away? I guessed he must be at least eighty years old. He always wore trousers, a light-colored dress shirt, and a waistcoat. That is what the Brits called it; in America it was a suit vest. And not just any vest, but a brightly colored brocade, or silk, or embroidered one. Paisleys, checks, and flannel patterns, he had them all. And most bordered on fluorescent colors. He must have had a closet full of them, as I never saw the same vest twice. The first meeting, while I was walking, he wore a bright yellow silk vest with purple elephants, reminiscent of a print from Thailand.

"Hey you!" I heard someone yell.

"Who me?" I answered, in front of his cottage.

"I don't see any other slackers on the road. Why do I see you walking around here all the time?"

"I live here."

"Bah. That explains nothing."

"I have lots of free time to walk?"

"Don't answer with a statement phrased as a question."

"OK, I'm a Russian spy tasked with finding old people to harass, forcing them into nursing homes and creating a burden on the government. Part of the five-hundred-year plan of world dominance."

"First plausible thing you've said. Come closer so I don't have to yell." I walked closer to his front porch. The yard had seen better days. I doubted he cut it every week. "Now don't step on the young magnolias, you ox."

"Sorry, I can't see them for the tall weeds."

"Wait til you get old, you won't be cutting the lawn like you used to."

"I believe it. I already hate cutting grass."

"How old are you? Shouldn't you be at work?"

"I retired early, as in very early."

"Repeating yourself already, I see. Early onset dementia took you out of the workforce."

"Not exactly, but close enough."

"So, why are you in my yard?"

"Because you said to come closer so you would not have to yell."

"That means come up on the porch and have a seat. Unless you have something more pressing to do. But as much as I see you out walking, I don't think you do."

I went up the steps and sat in a rickety chair. "I am James Wilder."

"Millard Masden. Now what are two old farts like us going to talk about?"

"Tell me everything you know about this campus."

"Oh, a smart one. I'll be dead before I could get out all my stories. Then again, you might be dead instead. Are you a story stealer, James?"

"I suppose I am."

"Good. Now what do I get if I tell you my stories?"

"I'll cut your grass."

"Fine, fine. Just watch the magnolias. I intend to watch them grow to maturity."

"Glad you are an optimist. Sixty years is a long time."

"One of my secrets is I have the fountain of youth in my backyard."

"And yet here we sit, getting older by the minute. Let's go jump in."

"Can't. You don't have a ticket. You have to be eighty the first time in, so that you always stay eighty."

"That is a crappy fountain of youth."

"It is, isn't it? Nobody wants to be eighty forever."

"But you will get to see the magnolias grow. If you have glasses."

Whatever test Millard gave me, I must have passed as I ended up cutting Millard's grass after that. I managed to spare most of the magnolias sprouting up around the yard. I convinced him to let me transplant the rest of the magnolias to the edges of the yard. Most of them survived. The ones that didn't and turned brown got mowed over so I don't know if Millard ever noticed. I never did find the fountain of youth in the backyard. Or maybe it was the fountain of eighty forever. Not a selling point in my view unless it was the fountain of eighty years old plus the health of a twenty-year-old.

When I got home I stopped thinking about Millard. Kat demanded attention, so I gave her lunch and a post-meal belly rub. It was a short one as she needed to get to licking. It took a while with all that fur. I left her to it and I started searching online county records for the land along the Pine Mountain ridgetop. It belonged to an LLC I had never heard of. Not unusual as lots of land in the county was owned by LLCs, sometimes set up by groups of wealthy hunters or land investors. If I wanted something more specific, I needed to go to the county office and peruse the records. But meanwhile it could sit a day or two. I wanted to brush up on campus history in relation to the letter I'd found in the bottle.

I had two books of campus history I'd bought at the gift store over at the Little White House. They were mostly pictures but did have some dates of when things happened. A few other books had big chunks of general history, mostly the flashy parts lauding the campus helping polio patients, or from Roosevelt's time of residence and treatment. I needed to go to Manchester and see what their library had. Searching the internet brought up small pieces of more detailed history, such as mention of a particular building completed and a grand opening, with lists of attendees. Or Roosevelt having his picture made with a group as a water system was dedicated.

I decided to weed out all the Roosevelt history not directly associated with campus. Sure, he was greatly influential as president during some noteworthy times, but that would not get me a campus history. Anything he did for the campus and when he was on site would be included, but I didn't need all the rest. Although the search brought to my attention for the first time that Roosevelt had three vice presidents. I knew about Harry Truman, of course, but I had not thought he had two others before that. There was probably a story there, but it would have to wait.

Roosevelt got polio in 1921. He came to Warm Springs in 1924 in an effort to recover. He purchased the springs and surrounding acreage in 1926. The Warm Springs Foundation was set up in 1927. Fundraising began and the former resort became a rehabilitation center. That meant physiotherapists, physicians, and staff were brought in to treat and manage polio patients. The original owner of my cottage came in with the first group of physiotherapists. The original town was called Bullochville but changed its name to Warm Springs at Roosevelt's behest.

The old Meriwether Inn was the original building people stayed in when visiting the healing springs. It was wooden and full of steps, both of which were hostile to polio patients in wheelchairs. The steps I understood, but apparently the threat of fire in those days terrified the wheelchair-bound. The Inn was torn down and the Georgia Hall was built in the early 1930s, along with other buildings considered fireproof. More buildings came in later, with an infirmary, chapel, brace shop and hospital. The small campus began growing at a fast rate., bringing in lots of people.

I stopped recording information because from that point on there was too much to keep up with. Names, dates, locations went from one entry per year to multiple data points per month. I needed to change my approach. I opened the door to the storage space and pulled out two white boards. These were my "brains" I'd used for nearly three decades when planning complex experiments, outlining complicated financial transactions, or tracking down someone that didn't want to be found. All parts of my former careers.

I could apply the same techniques to charting the history of this place. But I needed one more item. On the computer I pulled up a map of campus, enlarged it, then began printing out small portions of it onto letter-sized paper. I taped them all together and hung the crude map on the wall with the white boards. I already had two larger boards ready to go for the Tammy Wilkins investigation. My study was going to get crowded.

The tedious work began. From 1927 to 1945 there were lots of people coming and going. Doctors, nurses, therapists, staff, and patients. Some existing buildings were torn down and quite a few new ones were built. A large construction workforce had to have been on campus. Those were not recorded anywhere I could find, other than the architect.

Famous people visited, sometimes often. I capped the input at 1945 since that was the date on the letter. Things happening after that may not be relevant, at least in relation to the letter's contents. It also saved me a ton of work because of everything that happened and kept changing after 1945. Each person's name and information went on one board. Important dates went on the other. I used colored markers to indicate cross references. I marked where buildings had been demolished in one color on the map, and used other colors to designate the years new buildings were added. It was already complicated and I probably had less than a tenth of the available information charted.

Without a better indication of the letter's subject, cutting off adding anything after 1945 made sense. My primary assumption was that a letter dated 1945 would be about something that happened that year or something that happened in prior years. What I was afraid of was if the contents were about something not related to the campus. I doubted it, but it would make all this work unusable. But I would at least have a better idea of what happened here on campus where I now lived.

I made the compromise to not spend much more time on filling out the boards and map. I could come back to it if necessary once the letter was deciphered. Kat was sitting in the other leather chair watching me when I started, but she had long since started a nap. I touched her and she trilled. I looked at the mess I had put up and wondered if any of it would be useful. Sighing, I picked Kat up, and turned off the light as I walked downstairs. Up on my shoulder, Kat purred down the steps.

Beyond all the junk left upstairs, I went over what I had learned that was new or what was altered from what I thought I knew. First, the campus was likely larger than the town of Warm Springs by the late 1930s. It was for all purposes a college campus sitting on a hill in middle Georgia, that very few people outside Roosevelt's circle knew existed. Roosevelt and his wealthy friends dominated the boards and committees, but I could not determine if they exercised much control over daily life and work.

I finished the day preparing a garden bed on the side of the house. Kat was with me for a while, but I bored her since my toil did not elicit any chipmunks. She trilled her parting, raised her tail and disappeared around the corner to the front of the house. A bird feeder attracted squirrels as much as birds. She found their company more appealing than mine.

I finished weeding and spread hosta seeds, raked them in and covered the bed with mulch. I had a few bags of seeds collected from the yard in Asheville. We had extensive beds of hostas before the flood took most of them. It was likely wishful thinking on my part that the deer would not find and devour the plants. Maybe they would not come around this side since it was closer to the building next door. The police station had some activity at night as they came in and out on patrols. Then again, the deer might be used to the routine and not skittish. I would find out in the next few months.

CHAPTER TEN

Monday morning started off well. I woke up and felt like nothing was wrong, at least with me. I got out of bed and the sun was up and the birds were chirping, so that was good. Nothing bad on the tiny bit of news I allowed myself. But soon enough it turned sour.

I walked down to the cafeteria as usual. I spoke to George, said hi to Edna as she was at the counter getting food, and sat down with my light breakfast and coffee. A gentleman sat down across from me in his suit. Ison had told me his name was Benjamin.

"Morning," I said.

"You need to know that people on campus are concerned about a body being found," he said, without even introducing himself or a salutation. "We don't need people like you getting involved. It was a simple accident. Better for everyone if it stays simple."

"What, you'd rather her found by someone days later so it would not have ruined your weekend? Would that have been better for the woman? I know you and the administration don't want a body to be found on campus, but it was. It has to be dealt with regardless of campus politics."

"I see. You are going to be a problem."

"No, I try to solve them when I can. If that creates a problem in your world, maybe you should reevaluate your priorities."

"You don't belong here. You need to stay out of our business."

"The way I see it, I'm a property owner and taxpayer on this campus. You merely work here. You should stay out of my business."

He left in a huff. I had continued my successful project of winning friends and influencing people. Ison had come into the cafeteria and caught the last of the exchange. He sat down at the table.

"Morning, Ison."

"I would say good morning to you, but I doubt it has been considering Benjamin's tone and abrupt departure."

"I'm beginning to think I don't like him."

"He definitely does not like you."

"Yet I don't even know him. My reputation precedes me."

"Don't worry about him. I think it goes back to your cottage. My understanding was he wanted to buy it."

"He could have, I guess. It's a free country."

"He's a cheap cuss. I think he wanted it to hang on the

market so he could get a deal. He never expected you to come along from out of state and grab it."

"His loss."

"It was. And now you'll never know the pleasure of his company."

"Somehow, I will struggle and survive."

"I think you've offended him sufficiently that he won't talk to you again. How did you manage it? I should do the same."

"It is a knack I have."

Ison laughed and went on his way to do administrative things.

The day did not get any better. I got the call I was expecting. Agent Sims wanted to come by with some followup information or questions from my previous interview. Hah, I was getting the quiet woman rather than talky man. It was good with me.

I asked her if I needed a lawyer. She gave a nice deep laugh and assured me I did not. I suggested meeting at the cafeteria and she agreed. If I made her mad, she probably would not shoot me in public.

When she arrived, we sat at a table in the back corner, away from the few customers.

"We have identified the deceased," she began. "Next of kin have been notified. I believe Agent Wood and Chief Wilson finished that over the weekend."

"Are you able to say yet who it was?"

"Her name was Tammy Wilkins."

I paused for a second as I wanted her to think I didn't already know that. "I didn't know her, but the name sounds familiar."

"It is possible. She lived in Hamilton and was a realtor working there and in Pine Mountain."

"Yes, I remember seeing the signs. Probably from when I was looking to buy my house. I have a vague memory of a blonde woman."

"You have a good memory. But from your background I would expect that."

"Did a check on me then?"

"Of course. Our one and only witness, who happens to live near the scene. We like to do our homework."

"It is good to know the investigators are thorough."

"We try. Which brings me to the reason for my visit. Everything you said checks out. We might ask you to come to our office if there's an inquest. Lastly, we appreciate your help. Unless something comes up, your part in this matter is over."

"Ah, I see."

"What?"

"You are the designated one sent to warn me off. Probably the smart one. I guess that leaves Agent Woods to drive the car."

"I'm not sure what you mean." She leaned back, and the smile was gone. Trending toward less friendly.

"You checked on me. You think I might interfere with your investigation."

"Some people that know you implied something like that. We don't need help, so please refrain from any involvement."

"Won't you need my testimony at trial?"

"What are you talking about?"

"Sorry, I was getting ahead of myself. Won't you need my testimony at trial after you arrest the murderer?"

Bristly was a mild word for her look. Now she was all business. "The findings point toward an accident. Is there something you know we don't?"

"Not at all, in fact I'm sure I know a lot less than you do. But the little I saw tells me it was not an accident or suicide."

"I don't know what you think you know, but listen to me. Stay out of our business. If you don't, I'll arrest you for obstruction of an investigation."

"Second time I heard that today. But there won't be an investigation if you are calling it a suicide or accident."

"Stay out of it!" She stood up quickly and stormed out of the cafeteria, never looking back. My charm was still working. I noticed over the years I could often make people angrily leave a room. I was much less adept at getting them to stay and smile.

That went about as well as expected. Now I would have to get more involved, despite what Agent Sims said. Meanwhile, I needed to get the unpleasant taste of Monday out of my mouth. I knew how to do that. Physical labor.

An hour later I finished cutting the grass in Millard's yard and put the lawnmower away. He had a pitcher of lemonade on the porch waiting for me. Today's vest was red paisley with bits of blue and gold.

"Thanks," I said. We clicked glasses and drank. "Millard, what do you do for fun?"

"I'm eighty. Fun is no longer on my dance card."

"You are painting a bleak picture of old age."

"Not bleak enough, just you wait. Or better yet, die young. You've already seen enough life, haven't you?"

"There have been times I had that thought. But I keep on rolling along."

"That is what we all do. Then I got here, and now I wonder. I'm still here, but my friends and family are gone. Lots of what I was living for has left me."

"I can understand that being hard. You never got married?"

"Oh, sort of. When I was in Leiden, a forever number of years ago, I lived with a Dutch girl."

"She didn't come back with you?"

"Nah, too big a move. After that I just never got around to finding a wife. Too busy and too dumb I suppose."

"I was in the Netherlands for a while. I wasn't in the market to meet anyone, but I did enjoy my time there."

"I did too. What about your tales of women?"

"I married a girl from England."

"How long did that last?"

"Just over two years."

"She left you."

"Yes, she did. How did you know?"

"You are a literate fellow. I assume you also peruse movie and television shows."

"Yes, so what?"

"The fictional depictions are a reflection of our real society. How many of them depict the American leaving the foreign girl?"

"Thinking about it, I can't recall it happening. Except maybe for a couple of stories set in World War II. But that was because the guy got killed or shipped home."

"That is my point. It doesn't happen the other way around. Same with the Dutch girls. Then what did you do?"

"Few years later I met Emma. That lasted a few decades."

"And now here we both are, without those we once thought we would die with."

"True, but there's still hope yet."

He laughed for a moment. "James, you see that line of traffic coming up the road?"

"Nope."

"Me neither, because there's no bunch of women looking for an eighty-year-old doorstop."

"Maybe you ought to get out more."

"I would except for this bum hip. Can't walk more than a couple hundred feet. I get groceries delivered twice a month. Quit driving because I don't like it, and my hip won't let me sit on a bike."

"Then what do you do for, well, not fun, but to pass the time?"

"Come inside and I'll show you."

It was my first time getting past the front or side porch. The cottage was built a few years after mine, but those built on the outskirts of campus tended to be larger. This one had six large rooms on the main level, and stairs up to more rooms or an attic. Three of the downstairs rooms had been converted to libraries. Custom bookshelves filled each room and books covered them from floor to ceiling. Two of the rooms had comfortably worn leather chairs, with side tables and lamps. The third room had a wooden desk with a leather office chair.

"This is what I do most days. That room is philosophy, the other is medical and sciences, and this one is fiction. Need a little whimsy after the boring stuff."

I scanned the shelves in each room. Some titles were familiar, but many were unknown to me. I noticed some were quite old and the writing on the spines was worn away. It was an extensive collection and quite unexpected in an old cottage in the middle of nowhere. Obviously, Millard loved books and had created a bibliophile's dream.

"I'm impressed Millard. I doubt this exists much anymore."

"It's been my hobby most of my life. Lately it's what keeps me going."

"Hey, I just had a thought."

"Is it rare enough that you have to announce it?"

"It is not book-related. Do you ever get down to Mable's?"

"Heard about it but have not been. Why?"

"There's a person there named Lottie—"

"That old moll still around? Surprised she is still kicking. Now James, you need to stay away from matchmaking. I'm too old for a girlfriend."

"Oh, uh, I didn't mean to imply that." Millard grinned, letting me in on his little joke. "I was wondering if you wanted to go try the place. Lottie is a bit gruff but can be chatty."

"Don't I know it. We went out a few times decades ago. Timing wasn't good. My being mayor and her the County Clerk didn't help either."

"Oh, you already know her? And she was the County Clerk?"

"Yeah, we knew each other. And she was Clerk back when they did more than what they do today. Nothing happened in this county she didn't know about. Real estate deals, divorces, bribes, marriages, deeds, arrests, lawsuits, taxes. She knew everything, including most of what was going on in the neighboring counties, because they all talked every week."

"I had no idea. She never let on about any of that."

"The good ones don't. That is why they know all the secrets, including where the bodies are buried."

"Figuratively or literally?"

"Both."

"Anyway, if you want to go with me to the diner, let me know."

"I'll think about it. I'm not dead yet so maybe I will sometime."

"You seem a long way from dead."

"Not really. Death is a daily companion now, but it's like a comfortable sweater. Always there but not intrusive."

"That is an interesting take."

"Every morning I wake up I say to myself that I'm not dead, disabled, or broke, so it's a good day. Besides, death isn't the problem. Ugly dying is what I fear."

"Being sick?"

"Bad sick, more like it. Don't want the pancreatic cancer and six months of hell, or the big stroke and watching my paralyzed body turn to bedsores. Death is easy compared to that."

"I see your point. I'll plan to take a pass on the ugly dying as well."

"Best you do. You still pondering about that young lady found in the lake?"

"I'll probably be thinking about that for years."

"But are you going to do anything about it?"

"All I can, Millard, all I can."

"That's the best you can do then. Don't be too disappointed if it is not enough."

"Speaking from your former political background, I suppose."

"Yes. Politically, it will be best if it gets swept away as an accident and disappears quickly."

"That kind of thing makes me mad."

"I'm trying to make you mad. You'll get more done that way. Besides, I figure you've got about four days."

"How's that?"

"The state will move to wrap it up this week, release the body and bury her. Then it is back to business as usual."

"They could always reopen the case with further evidence."

"They could but won't. You'd be surprised how seldom it happens."

"I don't like the thought of that happening."

"You got a suspicious death. But no weapon, no motive, no suspect. Plus, a lot of campus, town and county folks thinking that the rumor of murder is bad for business."

"I understand all that. I guess I need to get busy. Or rather, busier."

CHAPTER ELEVEN

I had been thinking about the land survey on top of the ridge. If there were rumors or gossip floating around it would end up at Mable's. Specifically, it would most likely end up with Lottie after what Millard had told me. My course decided I went to the basement to unleash the grey ghost. It was just my bicycle.

Sometimes I rode my bike into town. I'd bought it in the Netherlands when living there and brought it back. It looked clunky and stodgy, exactly the way most people would imagine a Dutch commuter bike to look. It had a basket, panniers, and lots of places to attach more accessories and baskets. Yet it was a marvel of engineering, with oversized but lightweight frame tubes, gearing worthy of a touring bike, and built-in bright front and rear lights. I used it overseas for long commutes, grocery shopping, and carrying lumber and supplies when needed. Best of all, I paid not a dime for fuel or taxes in two years. The only downside was learning to pedal against the North Sea storms with horizontal, wind-driven sleet. That was not an issue in Warm Springs.

Lottie gave me a double take when I walked in early in the morning. She made her way over to where I sat at the counter.

"You aren't supposed to be here. Not only is it breakfast on the wrong day, you came in the wrong car."

"Are you interviewing for a job as my personal assistant? You can keep up my daily calendar, even be my driver, so I won't take the wrong car."

"Why would I subject myself to that torture? It's already tough enough seeing you every Saturday at brunch. Whatcha need?"

"Coffee and a story." I suppose she was thinking I was about to ask her about the dead woman. But not yet.

"Coffee is a buck fifty. Doubt you could afford the story." She moved behind the counter to get and pour the coffee. She slid the mug across the counter to me. "What story do you want? And what's the daily limit on your debit card?"

"I don't think I need that kind of story."

"You sure? I've got all kinds of tales worth money. Who is doing who, one case of who is doing what, and lots of examples of tomfoolery, thievery and woe."

"Nothing like that, at least not yet. Have you heard anything about somebody selling land up on the top of Pine Mountain?"

"Oh that. Yeah, that information is not worth anything. A plain old boring greed story has no value these days. Too much of it going on."

"So, you know something?"

"Group of boys from Atlanta bought that from the original family years ago. Them boys sold it to some lawyers from Birmingham, but it was a front for venture capitalists from Vegas. Might have been some others involved. I even heard something about a New Orleans group. Plans are floating around to develop it."

"I have to wonder how you know that."

"Keep wondering."

"It's a nice plat, and decent sized, but I'm not sure it's big enough to get all that attention."

"What do you mean, it's not big enough? There's two thousand acres up there."

"What? It can't be more than two hundred."

"Did you look on the other side of the road?"

"Well, no, I didn't."

"Somebody told me you were smart. I'm going to have to go back and set them straight."

"How big is the proposed development? The entire acreage?"

"Yep, biggest one yet in this county, so I hear. Resort hotel, condos, houses, pools, equestrian center, and an elementary school."

"That is too big for up there. There is no water, and no place to put septic systems in if it's high density development."

"They are going to run pipes up and down the south side of the mountain into the town of Pine Mountain

Valley. They have water down there, they'll just pump it up the hill. All the sewage will come down, and the old chicken plant that closed has a facility that will treat the sewage."

"Incredible. That will change the whole ridge."

"Yep. You want the good news or the bad news first."

"Ah, at this point it doesn't matter."

"Good news is, development is coming. Bad news is, development is coming."

"Thanks Lottie." I finished up and took the grey ghost back to campus.

I pedaled into campus up the long hill. As I got closer to the house, Bryan pulled up beside me in his official SUV.

"Hi James. See you got a new car."

"Hey Bryan. Gives me something to do. What's up?"

"I heard you had a chat with Sims."

"I'm not surprised she told you, but it wasn't much of a chat. She probably suggested you read me the riot act because I'm breaking four different laws and soon to be on my way to the big house."

"You aren't doing anything illegal are you?"

"Not yet. I'm not even sure how to do anything illegal in this case."

"Good, that absolves me of any culpability."

"Always glad to de-culpa folks. But really, why are they calling it an accident?"

"They are not officially calling it an accident, at least not yet. You saw the statement implying it was possibly an accidental drowning. Sims said you implied it was murder."

"Then I must have not been as clear as I intended. I meant her to understand it was murder."

"Oh, I bet that went well. She was still mad when she called me."

"I tend to do that to people."

"No kidding. I have to officially tell you to stay out of it though."

"I mostly will."

"I wonder what 'mostly' means coming from you. Please don't tell me, better I not know. You still think it was a murder?"

"I'm not a hundred percent sure it was. But it was not an accident or suicide."

"That does not leave much other than murder."

"Sorry, I meant it could be manslaughter, wrongful death, something like that. Or just plain murder. I can't tell which since I have not investigated those around the deceased and therefore don't know motivations that resulted in her death."

"I'm glad to know you have not done that yet. But I'm getting a feeling you will though."

"Maybe. But I can't yet, because even I won't directly interfere if it becomes a murder investigation."

"Glad you know that."

"Bryan, I do have something to ask you."

"Go ahead, the worst I can say is no."

"I assume there was an autopsy. If so, it would be good if the state lab could hold any samples taken for thirty days at least. Might be out of your control, but maybe you could ask."

"I can. I think samples are held for some length of time

anyway. Any organs, however, will be released with the body for burial."

"I thought so. The only other thing is maybe to have an extra lung tissue sample taken."

"Why?"

"She was floating too fast. There has to be a reason."

"OK, I'll try. Anything else?"

"Not that I can think of. For the next few days, I'll stay out of the way and see what the professionals come up with."

"I'm sure everybody will be happier about that."

"I know you guys are busy, but come over for lunch. I'm making sandwiches and I promise not to talk about or ask about Tammy or anything associated with the case."

"Sure, I'll do that. Maybe closer to one o'clock I'll walk over."

"Good. Have some sandwiches and sweet tea and take a break for ten minutes from all this."

"Thanks, see you then."

Bryan came over a few minutes past one.

"Sorry I got held up. Figured it would not matter since it was sandwiches."

"Nope, not a problem."

"What you got today?"

"Pastrami, shredded lettuce, farmer's cheese, some special pickles and horseradish sauce."

"You make all that yourself?"

"Everything but the bread and lettuce. It's easier to buy bread at Mable's. They have a nice multigrain, sometimes with cheese. Oh, and not the cheese. I get that shipped direct from a family I know in the Netherlands."

"Fancy. How hard is it to make pastrami?"

"Not that hard. The right spices and cooking it long and slow makes it nice. Problem is finding just the right brisket these days. Used to be junk meat, cheap and easy to find. But then all the BBQ experts started making brisket."

"Did you used to work in a restaurant?"

"Not since high school. Although food was a big part of my career. I just learned to cook what I like. One of the few things I do where I get to combine science and art."

"Well, whatever you are doing, it is tasty."

"Let's go eat on the front porch." As we waked through the living area, I noticed Bryan take a look at the bottle on the shelf. He didn't say anything, but he must have recognized it.

"Your boys playing baseball this year?"

"Yeah, and that keeps me busy when away from the job. Trish and I take turns ferrying them around to games. Glad that most are here or Manchester. Sometimes we go to Pine Mountain or Hamilton, but nothing further."

"That is good. I was worried you had to go to Columbus."

"Not until they get older. Or, god forbid, they decide to play travel ball. I mean, I hope they are good enough. But then we'd have to drive to New York, Oklahoma, and Florida on weekends."

"Ouch, that does not sound like fun."

"Most parents think it is torture. But if you want the kids to have a shot at college ball or the draft, these days it's a must."

"I missed all that. Can't say that I would have done it even if it had been a thing back then."

We finished and took the plates back inside to the kitchen.

"I guess these are your books, since your name is on them." Bryan had stopped by the shelf. I think he wanted another look at the bottle, but then saw the books.

"Yeah, my small contribution to publishing."

"Oh, you have three textbooks on food?"

"Nah, just a couple of chapters in there on cooking. And another on statistics."

"That is an odd combination."

"I used to have varied interests. Cooking and statistics tend to intersect at the junction of processing efficiency and food safety."

"The paperbacks look interesting."

"Not really, at least as gauged by sales. I've done some fantasy and historical fiction. History is more fun when you get to make it up. On the other hand, some of the history I've researched is so unbelievable no one would think it true if I wrote about it."

"Is that how you ended up here?"

"Partly. FDR came here a hundred years ago and created something unique. It is crumbling now, but it was a grand experiment. An island where the disabled and minorities had status beyond most places in this country could offer at the time. One of those pieces of history that is almost unbelievable. I hope the crumbling stops."

"Me too. It is a special place. How many different careers have you had?"

"Depends on how you count it, but several."

"What kind of background do you need for that many careers?"

"Anatomy, physiology, muscle metabolism, microbiomes, statistics, microbiology, spectral imaging and a half dozen other things."

"I didn't hear anything about forensics."

"I promised not to talk about that subject. But I've done many research projects on turning live animals into food to improve human health."

"What does that have to do with forensics?"

"Each of those thousands of animals had to be killed. And the effects of death on many different aspects of the animal's physiology required painstaking study."

"Oh. You do have an interesting background."

"Used to, but not anymore. How's the sandwich?"

"Great. Now I know why."

He did not say it, but Bryan seemed grateful for the food and respite from talking about the case. I thought it important to give him the break. He was a good enough police officer that work could consume him. If nothing else, I'd given him a half hour of time away from work.

CHAPTER TWELVE

I woke up to a sunny morning, so I went to work. The commute was short since it was the guest cottage. The floor was not going to rebuild itself. I put on all the protective gear and resumed cutting out what I hoped were the very last edges of the termite damage. Soon I would begin pulling out the sheetrock from the living area. Sometime in the past, the pine plank walls had been replaced with sheetrock. Now the old stuff needed to go. Getting rid of it also would make it easier to run wiring and insulate the stud walls.

I swept up what floor was left, then went out and got the wheelbarrow. Dropping onto the bare dirt that used to be covered by the floor, I shoveled up all the detritus and put it in the wheelbarrow. Once full, I rolled it out and emptied it on the growing pile of scrap that used to be the guest cottage. I had a small dumpster coming next week as I expected to be finished with the major floor demolition.

Kat was mostly unimpressed with the guest cottage repairs. When I first pulled up the floor she had been interested in all the old nest materials under the floor. I could not decide whether it was squirrels, possums, or armadillos. Whatever they were, everybody was now evicted. She quickly lost interest when nothing small and furry presented itself. All the activity had run them off. It was the same behavior for when I had been outside digging around the foundation. My efforts did not produce any rodent playthings for her, so she had left to study the edge of the woods. Summer was her busy time from all the grasshoppers in the yard. But the hot months were yet to come.

I pushed the wheelbarrow around the pile and back toward the guest cottage. Then I hit a bump and looked down to see the tire had centered and crushed a new fire ant mound. I needed to put out more bait before they overtook the small yard in front of the guest cottage. Something clicked, and I looked down again, after stepping away from the mass of furious little buggers boiling out of the ground. The tire print in the fresh dirt looked just like...

I put away the empty wheelbarrow and took a photo of the tire print. I would download it later to my computer, but I already knew what I would find.

After everything was put away from the cottage toil, Kat and I rehydrated inside the house. I then rechecked the photos on my computer. The first one showed Tammy's shoes on the bank, a familiar brand of a lightweight sports shoe. I had a similar pair that I walked in during warm, dry weather. I had them because of a bum heel, of all things from a yoga injury. They were also good for my knees. The tread on the bottom of her shoes looked nothing like the print in the mud. I downloaded the photo I had taken outside of my wheelbarrow tread. It was a near perfect match for the tread in the photo from the mud at the lake.

The possible footprint at the lake was no footprint after all, just as I thought. Tammy had been wheelbarrowed to the lake and dumped in. That would account for the impressions in the mud under the water that didn't look like footprints. Tipping her body forward, some part of her had hit the water and the mud underneath. Then she floated away and some of the mud impressions filled in slightly or were rounded out by the wave action before the morning I arrived. But I needed to do some confirmation.

I found my way over to the buildings on campus west of Georgia Hall. The groundskeepers had their office and equipment warehouse, or maybe garage was a better term. Although it had a lot of stuff besides riding equipment in it. It was quite a collection of mowers, tractors, trailers, drums, and boxes of parts. Plus, another wide section of smaller yard implements. I saw who I was looking for in the back.

"Hey Ernie."

"Hey Wildman. When are we gonna start the garden?"

"You know the state works in mysterious ways. And all those ways are slow. Ison told me the first funds were appropriated so should be any day now."

"That's good news. Have to admit I had my doubts they would fund it."

"Me too. I guess there will be a few potholes in Atlanta that don't get filled this week."

"They will survive. We had one on campus that took three years to fill. But I doubt you came to talk about potholes. I heard you were the one to find that poor girl in the lake."

"Yeah, I did. I only saw her from a distance. I guess Bryan or one of his guys had to deal with it."

"I have to say I'm glad me or one of my guys didn't come to find something like that. That would have freaked me out."

"No kidding. Say, I was wondering if any of you guys have been working around the spillway for the last two weeks?"

"No, none of us have done work there this month. Except cut grass. You know how this place is. No matter the time of year, we cut grass."

"What kind of tire tread do the mowers have?"

"Let's go over and look."

Winding around various things brought us to three large mowers. I walked around each one and looked at all the tires. None of the treads looked remotely like what was on the lake bank.

"Ernie, can I take pictures of these tires?"

"Sure, go ahead. But you have to say cheese first."

Two minutes later I had finished. "Do you guys have anything else with tread that looks like this?" I showed him a photo of my wheelbarrow print on my phone.

"No, I don't think so. Does not look like a big tire or a boot print. What is it?"

"My wheelbarrow tire, at my house." I knew better than to show him the one from the crime scene.

"We don't use wheelbarrows much. But there are two old ones back against the wall."

We looked at them, two extra-large barrows with double tires. All four tires had a worn diamond tread. Not a match for either of my photographs.

"Find what you were looking for?"

"I think so."

"This have anything to do with the girl in the lake?"

"Indirectly. You know that area gets a lot of traffic so there are lots of tracks. Hikers, dog walkers, bikes; I've even seen campus trucks driving around. I was wondering who might have been out there."

"You think it was us?"

"Nope, I did not think so, and I just proved it in case anybody asks. But I doubt they will."

"You are right. Nobody asks us anything. I'm surprised you came to check."

"Better to be safe with the facts when I start running my mouth. If I need to."

"Now you know facts don't matter much."

"They have gotten loose lately. But they still matter to me. Have you seen anybody with a wheelbarrow near the lake? Or have any idea why somebody would, like a night fisherman?" The lake was closed to fishing, but there were rumors it occasionally was fished at night.

"I don't think so. Not ratting out those that might be fishing under the moon, but if they were, they would not bring a barrow or a cart. Easier to run from the game warden without one, if you know what I mean."

"I do. I might have even had to sneak away from a trout stream in the past."

"Then you know to travel light."

"Thanks for letting me check around. I'll let you know as soon as we can start the garden."

"Sure thing."

Back at home petting Kat, I felt I had done my due diligence. At least to myself, I had proven there was a wheelbarrow out on the lake and it was likely what carried Tammy to the water. I knew I was taking a risk by talking to the guys before the investigation was concluded. But I doubted the state police would even consider the wheelbarrow print a clue.

I had a list of circumstantial evidence that I thought was enough to at least call into question that Tammy's death was accidental. I knew it would be a tough sell as the state authorities did not like to be wrong, and the local people would not be happy to have a murder in the community. They would sell it as protecting the family, but I knew their real reason. Nobody wanted a murder in town.

Any one of the details I thought odd by itself was insufficient to declare a wrongful death. State investigators would explain them away, and I did not disagree. But together, at least to me, the evidence was adding up.

The wheelbarrow print was no longer in question. The car being wiped down was another clue. The arrangement of clothes and shoes could still be questioned, but I'd bet a jury would buy it. A truck by the lake on the evening when Tammy went into the water, since I believed Millard to be a reliable witness.

Yet I did not know what to do with what I had. Bryan would be the easiest to convince but he was now peripheral to the case. I did not think Agents Sims or Woods from the state would listen.

I decided to try Bryan first. Perhaps I could convince him, and if not, he could tell me where my hypothesis was weak. He was just next door.

"Hi Edna, is Bryan in?"

"Yes, he's on the phone. Take a seat and I'll let him know you're here." Edna took care of the office, plus all the non-police stuff that needed doing. I imagine she could also do all the police stuff. A moment later she motioned for me to go in.

"Hi Bryan."

"Hey James. You coming to my office must mean it is something official."

"Not exactly."

"Oh, that is even worse. What do you need?"

"You told me Tammy's purse was in the car. What about her phone?"

"No phone. We still have not located it."

"Could be useful to show her whereabouts that evening."

"We think the same, of course."

"A realtor without her phone?"

"It seems unusual."

"A lot of unusual things are stacking up, at least in my brain."

"What else you got that I have not heard?"

"Are you sure you want to know?"

"I am. I may not be able to do anything about it. Or it

might not be relevant. But I do want to hear what you have."

"Two things new to add to the pile. The print in mud where the clothes were found."

"Yes, a presumed footprint."

"It's not. It is from a wheelbarrow tire."

"Are you sure about that?"

"Ninety-nine percent."

"Could have been the grounds crew."

"Nope."

"You already checked? And look at all their equipment?"

"Yep. But I did not tell them why."

"OK, what else?"

"Millard saw a pickup truck out near the spillway later on Wednesday evening."

"What? He could not possibly have seen that far. Plus there are all the trees."

"Except he has a massively powerful telescope sitting on his side porch. Most of the spillway is blocked by trees, but the parking area by the gate is not. I was able to see individual grass blades with the scope. Easy enough to see a pickup truck."

"James, those things on top of everything else sure do make me think something is going on. But none of those things will convince the state folks, in my opinion. As for Millard, why didn't he tell me?"

"Nobody asked him is what he told me. As for it being enough proof for the state, I thought not. Nor is that even my goal any more. Are you going to give that information to the state people?"

"I have to. It will be noted, but I doubt will be added to

the case as reliable evidence. A wheelbarrow print and an eighty-year-old with a telescope won't get much traction."

"I agree, it's not enough."

"They are about to shut down the investigation. Anything found after that is even less likely to be considered."

"That only leaves one path."

"Which is?"

"After the case is closed, I'll find the killer myself."

"The state police are going to love you."

"I live for their affirmation."

"I'll write this up and try to leave you out of it."

"Doesn't matter. If they need somebody to blame point them my direction."

"Be careful what you ask for."

"I'll take my chances. Do you know when the funeral might be?"

"I've heard Friday or Saturday. The coroner released the body yesterday, and it was sent to the funeral home in Pine Mountain."

"Thanks."

<h1 style="text-align:center">CHAPTER THIRTEEN</h1>

First order of business this morning was getting to Warm Springs and Mable's. Time to find out what Lottie knew. I received my usual warm greeting.

"Look at you, breaking your routine," Lottie said. "I knew I should have re-upped my insurance."

"How's that?" I asked.

"Must be a natural disaster coming, you being here on a Thursday."

"Lottie, I'm ready to find out more about Tammy and those around her."

"OK then. I'm taking a break in a few minutes. We can sit outside on the deck out back. At least have a little privacy. You walk around the side of the building and I'll meet you there."

"See you then."

I got a coffee to go and a pastry. I had walked downtown today so I would get my two-mile walk in. That was the justification I used to get the pastry.

As I came around to the back of the old building, I thought I saw Lottie toss a cigarette away. I wasn't going to say anything since she was older than me and could do what she wanted. Besides, foodservice was a tough business.

"See that you got something for the road," she said.

"I walked into town. Needed fuel to walk back. But I'm trying to find out what I can about Tammy Wilkins."

"You should know I don't normally talk about folks. But that girl is dead. Now you been dogging that girl's death and didn't let go. Unlike those weak lilies from the state."

"What?"

"That girl's murder. Everybody else is too busy trying to bury her and the real story. But you haven't let it go."

"Guess I'm stubborn that way."

"Like a donkey or its cousin, the ass. But either way works. Makes me think there is hope for you after all."

"Besides just being an old donkey."

"Yep. Are you going after the killer?"

"First, how do you know it's a murder? Second, I'll let the police do their thing before I decide that."

"They're useless and you know it. Any day now they will walk away from it. Yeah, you'll be going after him alright."

"You think it is a him."

"Always is. A pretty and smart girl gets killed, no way it was anybody but a man. A woman would just run her down talk-wise. Some women might get jealous enough to take a shot at her if she had been diddling her man. But that girl didn't do that."

"From what little I know, she seemed normal."

"She was a nice girl from Hamilton, went off to school and marries her guy from high school. Kids, career, boredom and a boyfriend."

"OK, all that made sense right up until the end."

"Happens around here. You spend most of forty years here doing the right thing, sometimes your mind and body parts wander."

"Huh, a boyfriend. Didn't expect that."

"Cut her some slack. It happens around here a lot more than people admit."

"I think it happens a lot more everywhere than people admit."

"Don't doubt it."

"The boyfriend wasn't married, was he?"

"No, he was not. Why?"

"Just deleting suspects. No jealous wife."

"Nope. But like I said, women have better ways to take down a rival than murder in most cases. Now, there's stuff you need to know."

I had a feeling I was about to find out the quiet, slow, simple, small town wasn't any of that lately, except small. "I'm listening."

"Good. You have any idea of what you want to know first?"

"The husband. What do you know about him? Usually the first place to start when a wife gets murdered."

"I've known that man for years. He never had much of a

mean streak. Not saying he was perfect, but not like him at all to have killed Tammy. Makes no sense. But you need to check him out closer."

"You know anything about the boyfriend?"

"Not much, but definitely a snake. Drives fancy cars but doesn't leave a tip. I don't know what she saw in him other than he was somebody different and not from around here. I heard he dabbles in drugs and has a big house in Atlanta."

"According to Tammy's business site, her partner was a realtor named Joe. Local guy from what I found. I'm guessing you know him."

"Since he was a little boy. If the other fellow is a snake, Joe is a weasel. Never liked him. All smarm on the outside and being clever mean on the inside. Tammy knew him too, so I don't know why she partnered with him. Maybe because he brought in a lot of money. He was good at getting it from out-of-town people buying in down here that didn't know him long enough to see his bad side."

"How about Tammy? From everything I've heard, she seemed nice."

"She was, but smart too. Worked hard, good mom, had the usual problems. I think college opened her eyes to the bigger world. For some reason she chose to come back here and settle down. I think she regretted it some. Probably the reason for the boyfriend."

"I'll need to check on the boyfriend. And the partner too."

"She must have had a soft spot for that weasel partner."

"Think those two ever got together?"

"Not a chance. Like I said, she was smart. I don't doubt

he was sweet on her. But no, she would not have stooped down for him. Besides, I heard he was in trouble."

"What kind of trouble?"

"I don't know. Pretty sure it was money trouble. He and his wife made a lot, yet he was always short of cash."

Interesting. Maybe he was into drugs and needed cash. Could he have tried to blackmail Tammy about her boyfriend? There were a dozen reasons he had money problems, and a dozen ways he might have tried to fix it. But not many would be important enough to commit murder. "I hear what you are saying. Based on what you do know, would you suspect the boyfriend or the partner?"

"It's a toss up, so flip a coin. But probably a no on the husband. But if she taunted him about her boyfriend, it's possible he snapped."

"Thanks Lottie, you just gave me a few weeks' worth of work."

"Well, what are you waiting for? Get out of here and go get that killer."

"Yes ma'am."

My pleasant walk home was filled with a trio of potential murderers. Who knows, maybe two of them teamed up to do it. I understood what Lottie was saying, but I needed to check on the husband anyway. If only to get a read on him. Then I could address the other two men.

The official announcement was made at noon. Bryan sent me a text. It was a week since the body was found so I was expecting it. State investigators found that Tammy Wilkins of Hamilton died from a tragic drowning accident. The funeral was to be held on Saturday in Pine Mountain.

I was at home and working on some notes when my phone rang.

"This is Agent Sims calling for James Wilder."

"That sounds official."

"The investigation in to the death of Tammy Wilkins has been concluded. The death was ruled an accidental drowning. We found no evidence of wrongful death."

"So that is it."

"It's over as far as we are concerned."

"I don't think it was the right decision."

"Whatever you think you know, you have every right to believe it. But remember that you have no right to harass anyone with your beliefs. That will get you a visit from us and a restraining order from a judge."

"A hypothetical question. What if I am right that the death was not an accident?"

"We don't deal with hypothetical scenarios. We work with motives, suspects, and weapons. All the tangible evidence required to build a case, if there is one. You also need to stay out of this because any evidence you collect will be considered tainted and likely unusable."

"I'm getting the feeling you would rather I not get involved."

"I'm telling you to stay out of it. We can't order you to do just that, but I would highly recommend that course of action."

"You mean inaction."

"Whatever, just stay out of our business."

"Yet as a resident of this campus and a taxpayer in this town and county, it is my business if a body is found in my neighborhood. Something that I recently told someone else."

"Chief Wilson passed on your attempts to find evidence. We were not amused. Those things are not real evidence. Stop your delusions and get help."

"I appreciate your professional opinion as an unlicensed psychologist. Good day Agent Sims." I rudely ended the call. Then I followed her advice to get help. I rubbed Kat's belly for ten minutes in the sunlight out front. It was enough to get over the bad taste from the call.

I was craving a salad from the cafeteria, so I went over to get one.

"Hi George."

"Hi James. Just the salad today?"

"That should do it."

"I heard the garden is about to start."

"Me too. Just in time to get ready for summer crops. We will miss the spring greens planting."

"That's OK. Just throw in some extra squash and okra. We can always use those."

"Will do. Maybe next year we can expand and get a corn crop in."

"That would be nice."

"You should join us."

"I will if I can get my schedule worked out. There are a couple of tomato varieties I want to try."

"That is great. We can never have too many tomatoes in the summer."

"You know it."

On the way home, Bryan zipped by in the campus police buggy. It was a fancy side-by-side four seat UTV with blue lights. An open air buggy that was perfect for a spring day. They had it because they also had to patrol in the woods and sometimes check on hikers. He spun around on the road and came back.

"Hey James, want a ride home since you're carrying that heavy salad?"

"That would be quite chivalrous of you, Bryan. But I've only another forty yards to go."

"That's OK. I was going to take the long way around."

"Ah, a ride-along. Sure."

I climbed in and we went by my house, heading toward either the lake or the long outer loop. It felt nice having the warm spring air hitting me in the face with all the smells of wisteria and daffodils.

"I told Sims and Woods what you told me. They were not happy, just as we thought, and she said she was going to call you."

"Yeah, she did. I'm now sure she does not like me. Especially after I hung up on her."

Bryan laughed. "I wish I could have been there for that. I doubt anyone has ever done that to her."

"With her personality it probably happens twice a week."

"She really isn't that bad most of the time."

"I thought the same thing. She seems more intelligent and thoughtful than Woods by far. This case must be stressing her."

"My thoughts exactly."

"Is she from around here?"

"Not sure. Maybe Talbotton or around there."

"I wonder f she knew Tammy or her family. Or maybe the real estate firm."

"I don't know, maybe. But it does not matter now."

"No, it does not."

"So what are you going to do now?"

"I had a couple more thoughts I wanted to ask you."

"Go ahead."

"In general, how many women have you noticed that back their big car into a parking spot?"

"Almost none."

"It is mostly a male thing. Means nothing by itself…"

"But along with all the other small issues, maybe it matters."

"Also, did any of the night patrols see Tammy walking? Or notice a pickup truck over by the lake?"

"No, nothing was reported."

"The driver of the truck could have kept watch and timed it to miss them."

"It is possible. Is that it?"

"Yep, just checking more details. When you don't know exactly where to start or where to end, sometimes all the details point you in the right direction. I realize I've been operating on a misconception. I thought all I needed to do was put together enough convincing evidence this was murder. That would trigger further tests and investigations that would add even more evidence before samples degrade or the body was interred."

"That didn't work out. You know they won't reopen the case short of a confession."

"I realize that. That portion is done. But I can rule out suspects until I find who killed Tammy. And find the motive. Maybe not a confession, but a case strong enough to reopen and prosecute."

"Maybe. It's still a stretch. Do you have any indication who did it yet?"

"No idea. But I think it is a short list. Not that it matters at this point. I need to establish it was a murder first since some don't think so, or perhaps don't want it to be true."

"I'm not supposed to get involved in an official capacity. But if you get close to someone and need help or find yourself in trouble let me know."

"Thanks, but I plan to leave you out of it. No reason to get you into trouble."

"Still, I'm next door if you need me. Now I'll get you home before that salad wilts."

CHAPTER FOURTEEN

I decided to switch up my walking plans and get off campus for the nice spring day. I drove over to Pine Mountain, where Pine Gardens was located. It was a resort that provided tourists with a lot of options for recreation. The resort boasted golf, water skiing, and seasonal attractions like Christmas light displays. It was a nice place to go walking or biking with miles of trails. It also had two golf courses. The original plan was for Emma and me to play a leisurely nine holes once or twice a week in the off season when few other golfers were around. I had been a decent golfer once, and I planned to teach Emma. But now the plan would never happen, and I didn't like playing alone. I didn't like walking alone much either, but at least there was no obligation to be social when walking. When playing golf there was always someone to talk to, from the guys at the pro shop to the kids driving the refreshment cart, and other golfers during play. Social was not my thing these days.

I parked in my usual spot near the Lodge and started my circuit through the woods and around the lake. All the trails were paved which was nice when the weather turned wet. Since they were dedicated paths I didn't have to worry about car traffic either. This time of year, the woods and garden areas were full of blooms. Tulips, daffodils, quince, forsythias, and some early azaleas down low. Higher up were deciduous magnolias, and a variety of fruit trees including pear, plum, cherry, and crabapple. And of course, the redbuds, misnamed in my opinion since the blooms were lavender-purple. The camellias were mostly done for the season and browning out. The least favorite of the flowers were the deciduous magnolias, as the blooms of many varieties had a certain dead fish smell.

It was a completely different feeling from walking around the Roosevelt campus and surrounding park. Pine Gardens was a resort so there were people, especially families. It was still relatively quiet, and as long as I didn't have to be social I enjoyed the sounds of the families and other guests. I had been like them once. For some reason seeing and hearing them didn't bother me or make me lonely. I went through the edge of the area filled with cabins and downhill toward the lake. I usually circled it once or twice, winding around on the trails on the edge of the woods. The lake at pine Gardens was much bigger than the one on campus, and busier, especially in the summer. The beach brought in hundreds of kids. Waterskiing competitions some weekends brought in lots of adults.

I got to the lake and stopped. Something important was nipping at the edge of my brain, but it would not manifest. I looked around at the people, the water, trails, bicycles, and kids near the water. What was it that was bothering me? I was standing in one place on the path and realized I was blocking traffic. Stepping back, I froze again.

According to the official story, most of which I disagreed with, Tammy parked her car and walked across campus to the lake. She undressed and slogged through the mud to go swimming at night. The mud... Finally, it hit me. The old Boy Scout Retreat camp along the back side of the lake. Although closed it still had all the amenities listed on the map on the way to the lake. Boat house for canoes, fishing decks built on the water, and a sandy beach. Was the beach still there? I rarely walked along that part of the lake, but I did remember seeing the beach. The police believed Tammy walked more than half a mile from where she parked over to the lake. Then she went into the lake at a shallow muddy spot. Why would she do that when she could walk another fifty yards and go into the water on a sandy beach? Surely she knew about it if she had ever been to the lake before. Once again, that did not make sense. It was not an earthshaking revelation, but was another small clue that the official story was incorrect. Not enough to overturn the official version but one more piece to convince myself.

After my walk, I sat in the car and thought about what to do next. Since I was already in Pine Mountain, I drove by the funeral home. I spotted a site where I could park up front but off to the side. It gave me a good vantage point to watch everyone come and go.

I then drove over to the real estate office where Tammy worked. It looked nice but small, exactly how I would expect a successful realtor office to look in a small town. There was nothing special about it otherwise. Two other ideas popped into my mind. The town of Hamilton was a straight shot not far from Pine Mountain. I would drive down and go by Tammy's home address.

Hamilton was south of Pine Mountain and the county seat. It was a small town, not much bigger than Warm Springs, unusual for a government center. But lately it had been growing, with a few large subdivisions being built, wildly inappropriate for the minimal infrastructure in place. But the road from the south side of Hamilton had recently been four-laned all the way to Columbus. People felt the Hamilton County school system was better than the Columbus system. So they moved to the sticks for the schools, then commuted to Columbus for work. For those and other reasons, such as a quieter life and lower taxes, people and progress were rapidly moving in. All the growth was still on the southern side of Pine Mountain, the ridge and the town, but I was not sure how much longer that would last.

Outside of Hamilton, I drove by Tammy's address, but could see absolutely nothing of her house. It was obviously on a big spread of land and away from the road. A great deal of expensive fencing fronted the road border. I would come back after studying a map of the area.

My second idea was about the big plot of land up on the mountain. Hamilton was on the south side of the ridge, so I could drive back toward Pine Mountain and then take the ridgetop road. It was the back way to Warm Springs and went by the land up for development.

When I got there, I parked on the side of the road and walked onto the big plot on the south side of the ridge. I saw some survey markers I had not noticed before. The views were really nice, at least where I could see out through the forest. A lot of trees would come down to build a lot of houses. The roads would have to cut down at angles and tons of dirt would be gouged out of that side of the ridge. If planned right, every house and condo could have a view. Surely worth it to destroy a unique ecosystem found nowhere else in the state.

Tammy was a real estate agent, and this was the biggest development planned for the county in a long time, at least since Pine Gardens Resort. I wondered if she was involved in the deal. If she was, would that be any kind of motive? If she brokered it, her commission would be a large chunk of change. But I did not see a motive there. I also could not think of other real estate agents murdered for land deals or commissions. It was not a priority, but I would look into it.

I changed up my schedule when I got home. Instead of eating in, I walked to the cafeteria. Friday nights were variable, sometimes with lots of local people and other times just a few students that had not gone home for the weekend. Tonight, it was more of an average crowd. I was surprised to see Ison sitting down with a plate. I got my mashed potatoes, green beans, baked chicken, and tea. Fried fish was also on the menu but I was not in the mood for it.

"Hey Ison, mind if I sit down?"

"No, that would be fine, have a seat. Wasn't expecting to see you here."

"Changing up my schedule, but I thought the same thing about you."

"Beverly went to Atlanta for the weekend to stay with her parents. So I'm eating here the next couple of days."

"Oh, I hope nothing is wrong." Bev's mom was moving into dementia and her father was having a difficult time keeping her at home.

"It's not good. Her mom is getting worse, and her dad fell this week. Lucky for him no major damage, but he's getting frail. This weekend is the discussion for moving them to assisted living."

"Sorry, Ison, that isn't good. Best wishes for Beverly's task."

"Bev has known it was coming. Her father too, even if he would not admit it. Now, I'm going to change the subject. What are you up to?"

"As usual, I'm dating all the eligible ladies in town, staying out of trouble, and making great progress on the cottage renovations."

"Incredible, three brazen lies in one sentence. I hope there is not a thunderstorm around."

"Yeah, I didn't think I could sell it."

"Stick to your day job."

"I'm retired."

"Exactly."

"Ouch, a tough crowd."

"You will survive. Now tell me about the girl that wasn't murdered."

"You may not want to hear the whole thing. But you've heard the state investigators ruled it an accident."

"Which is bogus even from my uninformed perch. I assume you will give it your full attention."

"I plan to. Probably won't ever be able to get the state involved, but I'll do what I can. There are too many unexplained coincidences for me to think there was not someone else involved."

"So, you know she was killed."

"Not enough yet to prove it. But somebody, a guy, was involved enough to plant the body and hide evidence at the minimum."

"And who would do that but the murderer."

"That is what I think."

"The campus and town are still buzzing about it. The good news is the conspiracy theorists no longer have you as the top suspect."

"That is a positive. Who is on the board now?"

"Bigfoot, aliens, and the county sheriff."

"The sheriff? Why is he a suspect?"

"Because people are crazy. He was on vacation that week in Belize. He's on the list because the conspiracy theorists don't like him."

"What did he do to make them mad?"

"You ever meet him?"

"No."

"He makes everybody mad. Just wait and find out."

"Nah, I'll pass. Sounds like we would not get along. I've been accused of the same thing."

"Nonsense. You only make fifty percent of the people you meet mad. The rest of us tolerate you."

"Thanks Ison. I strive for tolerable. Say, when does Bev get back?"

"Sunday night."

"Want to come over for Sunday brunch? Gives me a reason to cook up my peach pancake surprise."

"That sounds interesting. What time?"

"Come over anytime between nine and ten. I'll plan to have pancakes done by ten thirty."

"Thank you, I will be there."

CHAPTER FIFTEEN

Opening the door to Mable's I was met with the buzz of conversation and clink of utensils on plates and bowls. The typical sounds of a diner. As I made my way to the counter I thought the tenor of the conversation buzz change.

"You're back again, two days in a row. Guess that last dose of food poisoning didn't deter you." Lottie said.

"I have not gotten sick once since I started coming here Lottie. Despite what you put into my food."

"I'll be trying harder then."

"Check with the pathology department at the hospital down the street. I'm sure they can fix you up with something more potent."

"Thanks for the tip, doc. The usual?"

"Why not. Hasn't killed me yet."

"We'll see about that."

Lottie had already slid a coffee across the counter during our maudlin banter. Now she was off to put in my order.

She came back after the nearest person to me paid and left.

"You're getting famous around here."

"Thought I heard the chatter change when I came in."

"That it did."

"I was hoping to stay anonymous in town."

"Know what they say about hope."

"I've heard several. What is the latest?"

"It breeds eternal misery."

"Oh, I like that one."

"Figures."

"Why am I famous? All I did was find that poor woman."

"Yeah, it is more because you're doing something about it. What's next on your list?"

"Heading over to Pine Mountain."

"You going to the funeral?"

"Not exactly. But I wanted to be there to see who shows up."

"Good idea."

"Any other tips I can use?"

"Don't take any wooden nickels."

"Ouch, I have not heard that in years. How old do you think I am?"

"Old enough to know about wooden nickels."

"Touche."

"Watch for the boyfriend. Doubt he will show. If so, he'll be dressed flashy and usually drives a bright yellow Hummer."

"He's a stealthy one, huh."

Lottie laughed. "He gets called a lot of things, but not that."

"Thanks." I finished breakfast and drove toward Pine Mountain. My normal Saturday of cooking for the week would be postponed until tomorrow. Though I wished I was doing that, than where I was going.

I had never liked funerals. Other than seeing a few people I rarely saw, I could not think of any other thing about them I liked. The smell of lilies or eucalyptus, the funeral director's morbid-friendly greetings, the dead body made up and presented for three days to the public, and the brimstone-preaching old guy in a suit. I realized some of those things specifically applied to southern funerals and viewings, and not to all funerals, but I hated all the ones I had been to in the South.

Yet I could not miss Tammy's funeral. I was not invited, but I could have still gone into the funeral home during one of the evening viewing sessions since it was public. Or I could have walked in to the back of the funeral service itself. But I would not. My compromise was to stay in the parking lot during the service so I could watch who came to the funeral.

I got to the parking an hour early to get up front, but off to the side to give myself a good view of both the parking lot and the entrance to the funeral home. I didn't count on being caught out, but it happened anyway.

A car pulled up and parked two spaces away. At that

moment we were the only two cars in the lot, so my idea of going unnoticed was already falling apart. A man in a dark suit got out, noticed me, and walked over. I knew him as one of the funeral directors, as he was a regular at Mable's. My window was rolled down to enjoy the nice day.

"Hello, are you here for the Wilkin's family service?"

"I guess so."

"It is early, but would you like to come in?"

"No thanks. I really don't want to go inside."

"Excuse me for noticing, but I don't believe I saw you at any of the viewings. Yet I know you are local."

"Yeah, I don't do viewings. Ever."

"I understand. Everyone processes grief in their own way. Is there anything I can do for you? I can bring you coffee or a soft drink if you don't wish to go in."

"Thanks, but no." Then I had an idea. "Say, do you have one of those photo montages set up in the foyer? I wouldn't mind seeing pictures, but I don't want to be around the body."

"We do have a board of digital photographs placed outside the room, in the hallway. You can see it without being in sight of or anywhere close to the open casket. Come in and I'll show you."

I followed him in. Nobody else was around, so I could get in and out without being seen. I really did want to see the pictures. I had not known Tammy or her family and had no easy way of getting photographs. Social media was always a possibility if I was connected to any of her friends, but I was not. The only photographs on the internet were a couple of her business photos. The funeral director left me by the photograph board after again asking if I needed anything.

Displayed were the usual assortment of snapshots of her life, progressing from pictures of her as a little girl, to a teenager, two from the prom, and another at her high school graduation. Then two of her at college, one of which was her in a sorority picture. A wedding picture, then her with a baby, another of her with a baby and a young boy, then Tammy with two boys and the husband. A professional shot of her that I think she used for her real estate photo. She was a cute girl moving toward an attractive woman and a poised professional. All brought to an abrupt end for reasons I had not found yet, by someone yet undiscovered. My eyes teared up both for sadness that she would not be continuing her life and anger that someone could arbitrarily end it.

The director came down the hall and almost stopped. Then he patted my arm and kept going without saying anything. Surreptitiously I took out my phone and photographed the later pictures. I left the building and sat in my car. From the photos I now knew what her husband Robert looked like.

A few vehicles began to arrive. Then a large silver truck pulled up. A man and two boys got out, familiar from the photos I had just seen. I watched them solemnly troop into the building. They were here to get a last glimpse of the respective wife and mother before the casket was closed prior to the ceremony. I took a few pictures of the truck from the side. Other cars began trickling in, with a variety of people in suits and dresses spilling out and moving into the building. There was enough activity that I could not see everyone. But the ones I saw I did not recognize. It was a large turnout as the lot filled and later cars parked on the street.

Was her killer here? Maybe it was the husband, and I knew he was present. Or the boyfriend. But I seriously doubted he would be foolish enough to attend. The business partner was probably here to round out the suspect list. Or maybe the killer was some family member or business associate I didn't know about. The list was annoyingly long. But that was my fault for not winnowing it down. I needed to get more serious. It should be easier now that the state police were no longer actively involved. My talking to people was not going to be considered interference in an active investigation, so that was a positive result from a stupid decision to call it an accident.

I sat in the lot until the service was over. Just before it ended, I moved my car to the back of the lot where someone had left early. I did not wish to be noticed still sitting in the same spot. Not that anybody had paid any attention. As people came out, they milled around for a while. Slowly they worked toward their cars as the hearse pulled up front. A group of pallbearers put the casket in the car. Some people drove away as they were not participating in the procession. I did not want to drive in it, but I decided to at least go to the gravesite. Maybe it was some sense of owing it to Tammy to know where her body was going to be placed. In reality, I had only known her as a body, not as a person the way all the other people in the procession knew her.

The hearse pulled out of the lot behind a county police car. Somewhere around fifty or sixty cars pulled out behind them as an off-duty officer held up traffic. Once everyone was gone, I left the lot and drove toward the cemetery. I would be watching the graveside service from a distance. The cemetery was behind a large church just outside the city limits. It was one of the biggest and oldest congregations in the area, and the cemetery was proportionately large. I parked in the back of the lot by the exit. I wanted a spot where I could see the crowd gathered off to the side of the church. Thirty minutes later, I saw people moving away from the gravesite and back to the lot. That was my cue to leave. I drove back to Warm Springs, all the while thinking about what I had seen today. Or not seen, which was a solid suspect and a motive.

Those were my next tasks. Tammy was dead and buried and the police were going to call it an accident. Her killer was about to get a free pass. Or so he thought. The police had given me the gift of investigating on my own without interfering with their investigation. The worst that could happen is that I'd get a restraining order thrown at me. Or maybe get killed. Either way, it was time to investigate some suspects and shake things up.

Sunday morning early I started the food and drink preparations. As I told Ison, I planned to make pancakes. Not the dollops of bland batter with no taste and little texture, only made edible with good syrup. Although putting syrup on those pancakes was just a waste of the syrup. What I was making was a cast-iron skillet delight with European origins. A Dutch Baby or German Apple pancake. But I had modified it for my own tastes. I should give it a name. Drunk Baby Peach Cakes? It sounded terrible even to me and reflected my inadequate marketing skills.

Although the traditional recipe specified cast-iron pans, I did not use them. Years ago I had them but they always seemed to collect rust since I used them infrequently. I now used the updated version, where the iron was covered with enamel. Somewhat non-stick and dishwasher safe so it was easier to use and maintain. The only drawback was making sure it didn't go from room temperature straight to the broiler or hot grill. It had not happened to me, but supposedly the enamel veneer could crack.

Using the enameled pan, my pancake dish was relatively easy to prepare and still impressed guests, so it was perfect for brunch. When done right the dish puffed up like a balloon in the oven but deflated as it cooled. Caramelized peaches gave it a nice color and wonderful smell. Served in the enameled pan gave the simple dish an elegant presentation.

Maybe I should throw in a peach mimosa for fun. I needed something savory, or at least not overly sweet to go with the dish. I could do a cheese bread. Oat muffins were the current fad, but I hated those little bites of roughage. Those were only good for feeding goats at a petting zoo. Maybe sausage balls, if I could find good quality local sausage in town. If not, I could always do an egg dish. Not exactly unique or flashy, but usually eggs went with most anything brunchy.

And tea, I needed good tea. I had some English breakfast tea but was out of Irish tea. English would do. Or maybe not. It was spring, so I should do something springy instead. I looked up some mimosa recipes and decided to try that instead of tea. Brainstorming a variation, I came up with a juice concoction that would work with grapefruit or peach. But I needed to add a liqueur like orange or amaretto, plus a bit of raw brown sugar to take the bite off if I went with grapefruit. I tested one, made some adjustments, then made a small pitcher to go into the refrigerator.

I made the pancake batter and peach filling and put it in the refrigerator as well. The last thing, the sausage ball dough, was the easiest. My variation was a basic mixture of flour, salt, sausage, and shredded cheddar cheese and spices, including some red pepper. Today I planned to make them a little larger and flatten to simulate small biscuits.

Ison showed up at the door at ten. He came in and I handed him a grapefruit mimosa. I decided the peach in the pancake would be rich and sweet enough. There was no reason to replicate the peach flavor in the drink.

"Oh, this is pretty good. I thought it would be more tart and bitter."

"Have to choose decent fruit. And sweeten it up enough to cut the astringency."

"You use sugar or a liqueur?"

"Both."

Kat made an appearance to sniff Ison's shoes, then she went and plopped on the floor in the sun a few feet away. Ison had been accepted into the household.

"Nice looking cat."

"She will do. She keeps me around because I can cook. Besides, she knows if I die she can feed off my body for long enough for somebody to come looking for me."

"Do you believe the stories about cats eating their dead owners?"

"I don't. I would need to see a number of documented cases before giving it any credence. Internet stories and urban myths don't count. But I keep a cardboard box of dry food where she can get to it just in case."

"Prudent. I wonder the same about our little dog. I guess anything can happen in the right, or rather wrong, circumstances."

"Yeah, like somebody killing a realtor. Oh, that was harsh. I should have eased into it."

"No, it is fine. Should I ask what you are doing or leave it alone?"

"I'm slowly looking around at some things. Everybody tells me I need a suspect, a motive, a weapon, and a body. So far, the only concrete piece is the body. Got any leads?"

"I don't think so. I did not know her. Bev knew her husband's family, at least her parents. She may have babysat for Robert a long time ago. But we never socialized. She and Robert's parents were older than us, and Robert and Tammy were a lot younger."

"From what you know, what is Robert like?"

"Typical kid in some ways. Grew up on a large farm. Not long ago, he took it over after his parents went to Florida. Got married when Tammy came back and had kids. I think they are into sports."

"Sounds normal."

"From what I've heard, yes."

"Robert never got in trouble in school or after?"

"Normal pranks, nothing serious. Although at the Homecoming game his senior year in high school, he started a fight during the football game. Both benches emptied because he kept it going. Knocked down three players from the other team. No harm since they were all in full pads and helmets. He got kicked out of the game once everything calmed down."

"You have a good memory."

"We were there. High school football games are cheap entertainment, plus we keep ties in the community. We still go to football games occasionally. Robert went a little crazy that night, took a long time to get him under control."

"But that was a long time ago."

"It was. Never heard about him going crazy since then."

"Was Tammy at the game?"

"Oh yes, that is what finally calmed him down. She went onto the field and got in his face. Everyone figured they would get married after that. Then she went off to college. I think Robert was out of sorts for a while until she came back."

"He didn't go off to school?"

"No, he stayed local. Not sure if he went to college at Lagrange or Columbus."

"I better get the pancake started."

"Just one?"

"It's a big one and more than just a pancake. Come watch if you want to. Or wander around the house or pet Kat."

"I'm going to look at the house for minute. Passed by it a hundred times, but I've not been inside."

"Sure, look around. Brunch in about fifteen minutes."

I already had the simple batter ready, plus I had already marinated the peaches in bourbon and caramelized them. I poured them in the preheated enameled cast iron pan to reheat. As soon as the peaches were bubbly, I poured in the batter and set the whole pan in the preheated oven. I slid another pan with the sausage "biscuits" in beside it.

"Hey Ison, should be ready in ten."

I did not hear back so I went to find him. He and Kat were rambling around the yard looking at daffodils.

"You've got daffodils growing."

"Yes, I brought some with me and planted some more bulbs. I used to do tulips in the mountains, but the voles got them. I might try them here. They seem to do OK over at Pine Gardens."

"That is true. Bev and I drive over every April to see them."

"I was surprised the campus here does not have more daffodils."

"Why is that?"

"Lot of New York people of Dutch origin used to live here. Thought they would have brought and planted bulbs here."

"I guess not since I don't remember seeing them around."

"Food is about ready. In case you want to refill the mimosa."

"Good idea. Should I bring Kat in?"

"Nah, she'll be fine out here. We can eat on the back porch, so she'll probably come nosing around shortly."

Ison thought the pancake dish looked good. While still in the oven, I showed him the inflated version. Quickly after taking it out, it mostly deflated but gave off a wonderful smell. I shook the container of powdered sugar over it to give it a light dusting more for the color than flavor.

I took out the biscuits and put them in a towel and inside a basket. I took the basket along with the hot skillet, holding it with a heavy towel, out to the back screened-in porch. Ison brought our mimosas.

"James, this food is wonderful. How'd you learn to cook?"

"Self-taught. Picked things up over the years, including other countries, and modified foods to fit my tastes."

"You've done well."

"Thanks, glad you like it."

We talked during the meal mostly about campus and how we both hoped to see it flourish again. We switched to iced tea since Ison had to drive home. Kat did show up and I let her on the porch. After more sniffing and head rubbing, she wandered back into the house. Ison went home to pick up around the house before Bev got home. That left me the afternoon to catch up on my weekly cooking since I missed it yesterday. I enjoyed cooking when not rushed or trying to impress people. Since it was only me and Kat that was not much of a consideration.

Following along in the brunch theme, I made a large and thick frittata. Much like Mable's Southern omelet, my dish contained whatever vegetables, greens, and herbs I had on hand. Except for beans or potatoes. Put everything together with the eggs and cheese in the deep enameled cast iron pan and simmer for twenty minutes. Cut into quarters that gave me four meals. I could dress it up with hot sauce, sesame seeds, or even a thick teriyaki sauce.

I took a raw ham out of the refrigerator I had bought and put it on the grill after giving it a dry rub. Thirty minutes later I put it in the slow cooker. It would finish late tonight. In the morning I'd slice it up then put most of it in the freezer for later. But with fresh bread from Mable's, I had ham sandwiches for the week.

I needed vegetables, so I pulled out the broccoli, cauliflower and Brussel sprouts, cut them into like-sized pieces, drizzled with olive oil and sea salt, then put them on the grill for ten minutes. Bagged them up after cooling and now I had tasty vegetables ready to eat. My last task was to cut up the fruit. Then Kat needed a belly rub, so I took her to my chair on the porch, along with the last of the mimosa, and raked the Zen garden that was her belly.

Once Kat was satisfied, I went upstairs to my whiteboards. Tammy's husband, Robert, was a big guy as I'd seen yesterday at the funeral. Based on what Ison said, he seemed to have been a hothead at least once in his younger days. It wasn't much but went into his profile, and on the whiteboard.

Ison had come through and the initial funding for the garden was allocated. The first order of supplies had been delivered. There was no time to waste as spring was well underway, and it was time to plant early summer crops. We had missed the early greens season already. But first, we had to place the fence and the main waterline. Otherwise, the garden would feed only the deer.

The initial team was George from the cafeteria and Edna the police dispatcher. Ernie and Wes from the groundskeeping crew. And me. We intended to recruit others once the planting started for chores of watering and harvesting. But for now, it was grunt labor for us to place fenceposts and string wire. Then running flexible pipe to the site to connect to the drip irrigation we did not have yet. Thus, the chore of watering for the next two weeks. Once we got drip irrigation, life would be much simpler. I had an idea that might get us there faster. I still had a trip to Athens to make and I would pass by my old favorite nursery supply place.

Having Ernie and Wes on the crew was a bonus. They brought a tractor with an auger on the back from the campus machine shed. We measured and marked a large rectangle on the edge of what used to be the golf course. Not on the course itself, as there was still hope for it to be restored and put back in operation. Ernie placed the auger and drilled a large hole at each corner of the rectangle to a depth of thirty-six inches. He drilled an extra one eight feet from one of the corner holes, along the line of the rectangle. Between those posts would be where we put the gate. Then he took the tractor back to the shed to change to a smaller auger.

Meanwhile, Wes, George and I carried a six- by six-inch post, ten feet in length, and put into each of the five holes. Ernie returned and drilled smaller holes along the perimeter of the rectangle, every eight feet. We dropped in smaller round fenceposts in those holes. Those posts were also ten feet in length. Now that we had the perimeter posts in place, each was held in place while Edna checked with a level while another of us packed and pounded dirt in the hole to stabilize the post. It was nearly as effective as pouring concrete but much less permanent. Two hours later, all our perimeter posts were stable and seven feet in height. That was considered the minimum height to keep deer out.

The second project of the day was stringing the wire

around the perimeter posts. It went quickly as three of us nailed in the plastic wire supports and another two strung the wire. It was a plastic wire wrapped with metal, so it could be electrified with a direct current fence charger. Strands were begun eight inches from the ground and every eight inches all the way up to seven feet. Deer were notorious for finding gaps as small as twelve inches wide and getting into gardens. The wire was charged by a solar panel with a battery backup that we installed on one of the gateposts. Handy to be able to turn it off while we worked in the garden. It was the best deterrent for the four-legged robber browsers. The deer had ten thousand hunter-free acres to browse, so I didn't feel bad excluding them.

With that finished, the perimeter was completely protected except for the eight-foot gap between two of the big posts. Ernie and Wes were building a farm gate to put in place later. It was wide enough to get a tractor into the plot, but they had to build it to get it the required seven feet in height. Lastly, we had a five-hundred-foot roll of flexible black plastic pipe to roll out from the plot to the nearest water spigot. It was close to three hundred feet away and was an old water source for the golf course. One of the few spigots that was still in operation. We put the roll on back of the tractor and as it unrolled one of us stood on it about every sixty feet so it wouldn't try to roll back up. Ernie cut off some extra when he got to the garden and put a large rock on his end. Wes did the same back at the beginning where it would hook up to the water. They would come back tomorrow with fittings to connect it.

The day's work done, all of us but Ernie walked back to

the parking lot and began to leave. Ernie had to take the tractor back tonight. Then Wes would come back and plow the entire internal plot later this week, and we had a large trailer of composted manure due in a few days. Wes or Ernie would use the front-end loader to transfer the pile to the plowed dirt, then plow it into the dirt. After that, we would lay out beds and rows and begin planting seeds and slips.

We planned to start with the easiest to grow vegetables that were used in the cafeteria. There would also be rows of flowers. Some, like marigolds, were to reduce insect pests while others like zinnias would be put in the cafeteria to give it a nice look. Edna was a flower gardener and knew what would work best. I thought we had thought of most everything, but I knew we had not. But that was OK, we had a start and would learn and adjust as we went.

Edna stayed behind as we got to the parking area and George left. Odd because although I knew her from campus and Bryan's office, we were not particularly close.

"Mr. Wilder."

"Please, we are working in the dirt together. Call me James."

"James, I know Bryan trusts you. From what I've seen I think he's right."

"Thanks Edna."

"Despite his trust, you know he can't tell you everything that is happening."

"I know. I appreciate his position and won't compromise him anytime he's working on anything official."

"That is what I thought. But you know, everything that goes across his desk goes past mine first."

"Uh, OK. But Edna, don't do anything or tell me something that gets you in trouble."

"I won't. But when you need to know something you will."

"Thanks, I appreciate that."

"Let's walk over to my car. Now that everyone is gone, I have something for you."

She had parked in the old lot that once served a bustling and semi-famous golf course. Now mostly weeds and grazing deer at night. Edna opened her car and gave me a large envelope.

"Don't ask me what is in it. I don't know anything about it."

"Neither do I, Edna. But thanks."

She smiled and left. I ruminated about what I was carrying while walking home although I had a good idea what was in it. I doubted it would get Edna into trouble, but I would scan it into my computer, relay it over to the external drive with the photos, then erase the scans. The paper in my hand would become fuel for my back porch grill after I read it. I still enjoyed reading from paper sometimes.

That evening, I sat in my leather chair while Kat jumped up beside me, plopped down hard and turned on her back. She was demanding one of her several daily belly rubs. She got it.

Inside the envelope was the preliminary autopsy report. It was what I hoped to find. The official report would take weeks to get released and probably would be the same as what I was reading. I sped through the autopsy report, skimming the sections for major findings. Then I reread it slowly from the beginning. I didn't need any of the physical description of the body, other than she was a healthy adult with no signs of disease, accident trauma, or violence. The toxicology section was much more interesting.

Tammy's body was negative for any drugs except for the presence of ketamine. It was the new fad drug for humans that was quite old in veterinary practice. I had used it myself when performing operations. I needed to check into how easy it was to get it these days. Years ago, it was only available with a veterinary prescription.

The amount found was quite low and would not have caused death. That left a whole slew of questions. Did she take it knowingly, or was it given to her without knowledge, and where did it come from? It was an avenue that should point to the suspect. No alcohol or other drugs were found. I checked further but apparently there were no specific tests conducted for carbon monoxide or dioxide. Probably because there were no physical abnormalities that pointed to gas poisoning.

That pointed toward the boyfriend as he probably had easy access to drugs. Then again, those with a farming background like the husband could get it if they knew a veterinarian.

Reading on, there was no evidence of any sexual assault. No signs of a struggle as far as bruising or lacerations where she was held or tied. Nothing under her fingernails or any defensive wounds. Nothing obvious indicating foul play. So, she was not in a fight, strangled or tied up. But if she had ketamine in her system, it might not have been necessary to bind her. I needed to look up the dosage levels and how long it stayed in the human body.

My animal studies would not be relevant. Whatever happened, she must have known and not been afraid of who she was with before her death.

Asphyxiation from drowning was listed as the cause of death. But her lung weight and visual observation indicated little water in the lungs. That did not show a traditional drowning outcome. Maybe the coroner couldn't come up with a better reason. I looked into the notes and saw dry drowning was mentioned. I was unfamiliar with the term but would be looking it up.

Again, how did Tammy get that drug in her system? There likely was not enough to cause unconsciousness for long, or maybe not at all, and certainly not death. The major reason to use the drug was to initiate an assault against the recipient, but there was none. Even if she was unconscious from the drug, death would have resulted from drowning as her lungs flooded as she would have continued breathing. Yet not much water was in the lungs.

I dived into online research on dry drowning. The initial results showed some twenty percent of drowning victims died from asphyxiation when their throats closed up in the water, causing death without flooded lungs. That might explain Tammy's death, if there was a one-in-five chance of it happening to her. But the further I delved into the actual research, the more that fell apart. Apparently, that number was thrown around a lot, but when I pulled up actual scientific papers, the incidence of dry drowning was closer to two percent. A one-in-fifty chance it happened to Tammy. I had to discount that idea. But I had to come up with something that would explain how she died if she did not drown.

I also brushed up on the latest ketamine reports. I knew ketamine was widely used by veterinarians for anesthesia, commonly to spay and neuter pets. It was probable that every vet practice stocked it. I was surprised to find that it was now being used on humans for anxiety and depression. Wow, after seeing the effects on animals, there was no way I'd take it on purpose. But apparently it was now acceptable. Maybe it was more readily available than in the past. Which would not narrow down the source much. I looked up vet practices and saw several in the area, but none had a name recognizably tied to any potential suspects. Which didn't mean much since few were named for the owners. I would have to dig deeper and look up business records. Or was Tammy taking it voluntarily? Maybe she was self-medicating for anxiety. If so, I was not sure who to ask. It needed to be someone that knew her well but was willing to give up her secrets.

It was time to apply clues to suspects. Or at least the likeliest suspects I had. Maybe that would lead me to what I really needed—a motive. It was back to the whiteboard to set up my version of a matrix of clues.

CHAPTER EIGHTEEN

Despite the need to sift the clues for a murder suspect, I decided to take a day for thinking. A good way to do that was by driving fairly slowly on well-traveled roads. Sometimes my brain needed a distraction while doing something else unrelated. I made sure Kat was stocked for food and water, grabbed the message that used to inhabit the old bottle, and hopped in my tank. Older and four-wheel-drive, once luxurious, it still got me around most of the time.

Kat was staying home as she didn't like riding in cars. I would go up and back the same day as I did not want to keep her cooped up all day and overnight. She would be fine for several hours, but I didn't like leaving her more than that, and not often. I could get someone to come over, but it wasn't the same. Some things just came along with cohabitating with a cat, like decency. Besides, I had a love-hate attitude toward Athens and the university that was thrusting up through the heart of the city. I didn't want to stay there in a hotel.

I took the back way to Athens. It was considerably longer, but I was not in a hurry. I would not be wasting time, I would be thinking. Driving the Interstates for a few hours and through Atlanta twice in the same day was beyond insanity. Instead, I cruised through old Georgia towns full of history. Some good, some not. Woodbury, Meansville, Barnesville, Forsyth, Monticello, Madison, and Watkinsville. Even smaller hamlets like Molena and Shady-dale, and communities no longer even named once the mill or railroad responsible for their existence disappeared.

The redbuds were blooming and soon the pines would douse the state in the beloved yellow dust. Cars, sidewalks and buildings would turn yellow for days until the showers rinsed it to the ground, forming bright yellow puddles and streams. Pollen was great stuff, the gift that keeps on giving. But the drive was nice enough, and I was blessed not to have logging trucks pull out in front of me. The only disturbing thing was the lack of bugs. I remember driving when every fifty miles you had to stop and thoroughly clean the windshield. Now I could go all the way to Athens and have only a few smudges.

Just over two hours I neared Athens and thought about another part of my life that was mostly forgotten. When I first began graduate school, I was at a meeting and met a girl. It was a lot of fun of first, so much so we got married on a lark. Problem was, she lived in another country. It ended badly and my Master's program outlasted the marriage. I had not heard from her in more than thirty years, so I supposed she was happy wherever she was. A lot of life since then and Emma had put those memories down in the cellar.

I parked in the Georgia Center lot because it was possibly the only place on campus that had spots for visitors. Since it was the official university hotel and conference center, it had to accommodate visitor parking, for a price. I began the trek across campus. This was not the nicely-grassed and manicured North campus full of antebellum-columned buildings where the arches looked haughtily over the town. South campus instead was where the gritty work was done. Science and agriculture were represented by the plain, boring buildings divided by concrete and asphalt roads and lots.

The two campuses were divided not only by a stream and ravine long since paved over, but by the football stadium. A behemoth of concrete that was the most important edifice ever created, according to many Georgians. As a student, for me it meant tailgate parties and cheap entertainment. As a professor, it meant distraction and disruption, due to getting kicked off campus for two days every home game. My parking spot was more valuable to the university than anything I ever did in the pursuit of knowledge.

I arrived at the appointed nondescript building. Albert's lab was in a plain cream-colored brick building with a low boring hedge and a parking lot out front. Parking lots were everywhere on South campus because the spaces were rented for football season each year to wealthy patrons. Tailgating was now big business for local places and the university. I believed the hedges were kept in place as convenient restroom facilities for drunk fans. I knew all about it as a party-going student in the distant past. I possibly had made emergency use of this very hedge.

Inside I found the right office and knocked on the door. I did it gently, as I did not want any loud sounds to cause an avalanche among the wall-to-wall stacks of papers. It might take days to find Albert's body.

"Hi James, good to see you. How is retired life?"

"A bad day retired is better than a good day hired, or something like that."

"I know. A few more budget cuts and I'll be joining you. Now, what wonder did you bring me?"

I opened the folder and carefully removed the pages. "Here you are."

"I am going to make copies. One set for you and one for me. We should be done with the originals in a few weeks, maybe less."

"Thanks for running the analysis."

"No problem. It will be good for the lab. I'll be right back."

When he returned he gave me a set of copies.

"James, we will take good care of the original pages. There may be a few wrinkles or cracks since we will need to manipulate them a bit. But based on the quality and condition of the paper I'm holding, I believe any impact will be minor. When you told me the letter was in a bottle buried in the dirt, I expected it to be in much worse shape."

"Possibly because it was under a building, so it stayed

dry, and the temperature range was not as extreme if it had been in the environment."

"True. The paper also looks like a nice bond, very high quality. Not sure many places nowadays sell paper this nice. Probably why the ink faded; the paper may have absorbed it more than usual."

"Will that make it harder to scan?"

"It should not. What absorbed may even be better preserved, but we will know once we use some different backlighting. I'm sure we have enough options to find ones that work."

"I feel like this letter is getting the same treatment as the Dead Sea scrolls."

"If only. We would be charging you a lot more money."

"I thought you weren't charging me anything."

"We're not, so you might get what you pay for."

"Like that night in Atlanta during the conference in grad school. When you were talking to that friendly girl?"

"I had no idea she was a prostitute. You could have told me."

"It didn't matter, you did not have any money, anyway. She would have realized that soon enough."

"Still, I would not have wasted my time. I could have been talking to an actual date."

"Come on Albert, we went to what, a dozen of those meetings? Name one time either of us spent time with a girl we met there that lasted past one conversation."

"True enough. But that night could have been the one time it was going to happen."

"Yeah, and that letter you are about to decipher is a treasure map to El Dorado."

"If it is, you'll never know it until I invite you to my private island estate. Oh wait, I do remember that conference in Arkansas. Didn't you meet a girl there? I thought that was serious."

"You have a good memory. But it didn't last."

"Oh well. I thought you two got married for a while. But I guess not, since you were married to Emma for so long."

"We did, and it did not. I need to go, Albert since I'm driving back."

"Nice to see you James, drive safe. I'll give you a call when we're done."

"Thanks again Albert."

On the drive back, I stopped in Watkinsville at a coffee shop I had frequented for years. I had lived in both Athens and Watkinsville several times in the past for different reasons. Somehow the coffee shop had survived and even had other locations. They had great fresh beans since they roasted them in Athens. Whenever I stopped I always thought there was a chance I might meet someone from a former life there, but to date that had not happened. The coffee was still good, so I always pulled in for a cup. One while there and one to go. Or maybe I was just used to buying two cups from days past.

After coffee, I visited my old favorite irrigation store. I picked up a roll of black plastic tubing and a few handfuls of fittings. The tubing and fittings would allow us to configure pieces of tubing to follow every row of growing crops and not waste water. I also bought several packages of emitters. Those were tiny valves that metered water out a gallon per hour, or whatever amount was needed, as there were multiple options. The emitters were on the tubing so the water was sent directly into soil, exactly where it was needed. Simple and efficient once the system was put in place. That would be our next group activity.

I traveled on to Madison. Sometimes I drove through the old town instead of the bleakly overdeveloped bypass highway. Today I went through town. The old houses spared by Sherman were almost all in great condition. Today the old beauties were sporting their spring colors. All the early azaleas were out and the dogwoods were on the verge of popping. A few had already broken open. On the ground various pastels of yellows and soft whites were anchored by the daffodils or jonquils. I could never tell the difference. A couple of yards even had tulips which made me think of the years Emma and I had spent in the Netherlands.

We used to come to Madison for the Christmas parade of homes. I hadn't thought about that in a while. Must be having one of those nostalgic flashbacks. The mood had nudged me in Athens, but really kicked in after buying two coffees in Watkinsville. I needed to get home and work on the guest cottage, Tammy's murder, or something, anything. Keeping busy kept me from thinking about my own life.

I continued driving and began going back over Tammy's case again but did not come up with anything new. I definitely had enough anomalies to know it was murder. It would never get the state police to change their mind, but they could not say they didn't know.

Driving into campus and home, my thoughts shifted back to the letter. I would give it more thought in the morning. Now it was time for some tea and hang with Kat. I went outside with her and we prowled along the edge of the woods, but no rodents cooperated. She had fun anyway. While outside, I studied the guest cottage and made plans for a covered porch to replace the tiny stoop. We went inside for dinner and after I went for a walk around campus. It was a good way to detoxify from being in a car for five hours. Then I ate dinner and settled in the chair with Kat. I already owed her two belly rubs, so she had to settle for one, but for extra time.

CHAPTER NINETEEN

The husband, Robert, was a local farmer and ran a business that I had not researched. His family went back several generations. I guess that accounted for his extensive land holdings. I had never met him but remembered passing by the huge spread of land in Hamilton when I drove by. It was distinctive from the expensive and extensive fencing around it. One of those places where the fence ran along the road for a mile. I looked at the satellite map of the spread, and noted a large house, but not nearly as big as I expected. The barn was bigger than the house, so it must have been an actual farm. Usually a place that big was all house and no barn, built to impress whoever was special enough to be invited past the fancy gate.

The man did not seem like the type to murder his wife. But that was likely said about half the wife-killers in the world. If he was enraged, then maybe. But sneaking around and slipping her into a lake didn't fit from what little I knew.

The partner, Joe, seemed legitimate in regard to his realty business. He was local, so I could ask around about him and see what skeletons might rattle around in his pantry. I also had a plan to get to know him if I had to.

The boyfriend, Larson, was a more interesting case. I had searched for him on the internet and called up a retired policeman I knew in Atlanta. What I knew so far was not much. He lived in Buckhead, a very upscale area near downtown Atlanta. He had a reputation as a playboy. Expensive cars, two DUIs, and, according to some rumors, was a drug entrepreneur. I had no idea how Tammy had met him, unless he had come down to look at a property. Apparently, he was a hunter in his spare time, and Hamilton County was known for its hunting opportunities. He owned a gym in Buckhead. I wasn't sure it was lucrative enough to pay for his lifestyle. I needed a closer look at Larson the boyfriend. Unfortunately, a trip to Atlanta was necessary. Today was the day. I plugged the home address into my phone GPS and took off.

He lived in a nice house. It set back off the road with a long driveway. A three-car garage had been added on the side of the house. It looked like a typical expensive home for this part of town. Nothing stood out. I also abandoned thoughts of going around the house and possibly going inside. There was no easy way to do it without being noticed or getting away easily if something went wrong. I was not going to fake being a utility contractor, either. It worked for television, but I did not trust it in real life.

I went to the gym, went in and asked for a tour at the counter as a prospective member. The attendant was not overly eager to do so, as I soon realized I didn't fit the member profile. Inside were mostly females in spandex outfits. Fifteen minutes later I knew absolutely nothing more than I had when I came in, other than there were a lot of attractive women present in the middle of the day. The place must be doing well. There were also cameras everywhere so now my face had been recorded.

The trip had been unsuccessful. I knew nothing about the boyfriend nor his relationship with Tammy. I thought about contacting him directly and perhaps posing as a bored private detective working for the family. But that would not get me anywhere if he was a smart guy. He probably would not admit to the affair. Even if he did, I doubted he could tell me Tammy's reasoning for doing it, as he probably did not know. And it may have had nothing to do with her murder anyway.

I continued to think about other ways to check on the boyfriend. Talk to friends, family, or business associates probably would not work. No reason for them to talk to me and even if they did, they likely would not know the information I was looking for. I would have to approach it differently. Especially since talking to him or his people might be interfering with a murder investigation if the case was reopened. I didn't know if the police knew about the affair and whether they had talked to him. Regardless, I had to be careful.

I drove away from the concrete monstrosity that was

eating north Georgia. It was where I once lived as a child, but I had escaped and never wanted to move back. The city had an allure to some, but I did not see it.

I made it back to Warm Springs and parked in front of Mable's. They were just closing for the day after serving lunch. It was perfect timing for what I needed. It was a pleasant day so I leaned against my car in full view of the diner's windows. A few minutes later, Lottie came out.

"Is this a stickup?" she asked. "Or are you stalking me?"

"Probably the latter. I just got back from Atlanta."

"My condolences. Nobody would go there on purpose."

"I needed to check on Tammy's boyfriend."

"Oh."

"I got nothing. Nor did I figure out a way to get anything useful."

"Other than what I told you, I don't know any more."

"That's OK. But maybe you know if Tammy had a best friend, someone she confided in."

"There is someone she probably told everything to. But she might not talk to you. Oh, that is why you're harassing me."

"Exactly. Will she talk to me if you are there, or at least talk to you and you can ask her some of my questions?"

"Maybe. I should know by tomorrow."

"Thanks."

I had plenty of daylight left, so I decided to follow up with my thought from the day before. I could do more research on the letter's time frame of history easily enough.

I had spent some effort learning about campus history before and during the time the letter was written. There was some information on people, but it seemed focused on the famous visitors, plus there was a lot about the buildings and events held on campus. Not as much on the people who lived and worked every day on campus. I realized there was one place nearby that could have some pieces of history that I didn't have yet. Otherwise, I'd have to go to south Atlanta or New York to dig out arcane details from the archives.

Once as a kid I had been to the Little White House. One side of my family was from the town of Talbotton, about an hour away to the south. On a trip there when I was about six years old, we visited the Little White House on the way home to Atlanta. Other times more recently I had been to walk or to look at the architecture and fireplaces to get an idea of how to renovate the guest cottage and keep it in the period style.

I remembered a number of displays about the grounds and people that might be helpful. At least local names I could research. Unfortunately, I had ignored most of the displays on the previous trip. To get in for free, I drove over to the Manchester public library and got a free entry pass. I could have also gotten a free parking pass, but I would walk from my house. Free passes were a little-known benefit available to users of the state parks. It was worth the four-mile drive there and back.

I walked up to the Little White House and went in the back gate. Going into the museum building, I slowly browsed through the small keepsakes like tea sets and canes over to the large displays like Roosevelt's car and a horse carriage. I managed to see everything and read the captions. Next stop was the Little White House itself. Interesting but not exactly useful to my quest to understand the Roosevelt campus. Heading back to the museum, I looked into the building in front of the Little White House that had a garage underneath. It was built to house his cook, Daisy Bonner, along with his valet and maid, Irving and Lizzie McDuffie, respectively. Daisy was local, while the McDuffie's traveled with him. I wrote down their names to look up later. The little upstairs space must have been cramped for three people.

Scattered around the grounds, I saw several small wooden stands where marine guards were stationed when Roosevelt was on the property. I did not see any housing, nor did I remember seeing it mentioned in the museum. The marines must have been quartered somewhere. I asked a museum employee and found out there was a barracks near where the lake and old camp now was. That was interesting as they would have had some access to campus. I made a note to look for further information on them.

To be thorough on my informal research trip, I entered the gift shop. Again, I saw little I had not already seen or already knew about. There was one book I didn't have so I bought it. Flipping through it I saw a picture of Roosevelt, Bobby Jones the golfer, and a few other people, including the original owner of the cottage I now owned. The campus hosted famous people, but it was a small world. Altogether, the Little White House was very interesting but not on point to gather details about the early years of the campus.

The visit had not accomplished my goal but had stirred up memories about my past and family. Mine, which were some distance away. But also Emma's family, who lived relatively close. Her parents were from a town about an hour away in the other direction from mine. But she had two elderly aunts and some cousins closer to our age in the area. I had not kept up with them since Emma's passing. I should already have gotten in touch with them.

CHAPTER TWENTY

I met the woman at Mable's on Thursday as they were closing. Lottie introduced us, and we sat in a booth. Lottie did not sit with us but was nearby, wiping tables and filling salt shakers after the last customer left. Cindy Lewis was a local girl and Tammy's best friend for most of her life.

"Cindy, thanks for talking to me today."

"Lottie says you found her. Then when they wanted to make it go away, you tried to get them to look again."

"I did find her I guess."

"Why are you doing this?" I could tell from her face that my answer was important to her.

"I thought it was the right thing to do. For her sake, if nothing else. She was not a suicide, or on a silly lark to skinny dip. But in a way it's not about me. I was supposed to move here with my wife, but she died. If she was alive, you would be talking to her, as she would push hard to find out what happened and who killed a woman, even if she didn't know her. I guess I'm doing this for her. Sometimes it seems I hear her talking to me, and she is saying somebody killed Tammy and they need to be found and punished."

"I hope so. What did you want to talk about?"

"When somebody does this, it is for a reason. I know the case is closed, but I need to take a look at anyone that might have had a reason to harm her. Including her husband, if for no other reason to rule him out."

"I've known him as long as I've known her. He wouldn't have killed Tammy." I noticed she slipped into present tense in speaking of Tammy. She had not yet put her away into past tense.

"I agree. Everybody has their limits, but he doesn't seem the type." I didn't tell her I thought he could have killed her in a moment of rage, but he was not the type to lure her to a lake and make it look like a suicide.

"He's not."

"Then somebody else had a reason. There is a lot of evidence that she had a boyfriend."

"I'm not sure I should talk about it."

"I'm not interested in making Tammy look bad. I just want to know more about him, or maybe what she thought about him. If he was involved in her death, that part needs to come out."

"OK, I'll tell you what I can."

"Thanks."

"I've known Tammy since elementary school. We've been friends ever since. After graduation we went to college together and were in the same sorority." Cindy was going back over old memories, but I thought it best to let her. She would get back to the boyfriend soon enough.

"What was she like in college?"

"Normal. She studied and did well in classes. We did the usual dumb college things. But she stayed out of trouble."

"Nothing controversial?"

"Lord no, that wasn't Tammy. The craziest thing she did was join one of those environmental groups because she was always talking about saving the animals or insects or whatever. She did date some but nothing serious."

"What about after college?"

"Afterward she came back here and got married and had kids. I went to Florida, got married and had a kid, which ended that marriage. I moved back here and married a guy from school that didn't last two years. My son and Tammy's oldest play baseball together. I'm telling you this so you know we were close. She helped me through two divorces."

"I think I understand. Did she tell you much about her marriage?"

"Some. They were happy for a while, but things got dull. Small town girls like us, we like the stability. But we get bored like everyone else. Some spend their time with their kid's sports, some in church, some with work."

"Did Tammy get bored and find a boyfriend?"

"It was not like that, not really. She did not tell me anything at first, but I knew something was going on. She talked different, had a different attitude. We were out on a girl's night and had drinks. When the others left she told me about a guy she had met. She had shown him some property. He was from Atlanta and had money, she said. She did not do anything at first, but he was real persistent. She said he made her feel like a teenager again."

"Was she in love with him?"

"She fell quick once it happened, but it was infatuation. She got over that just as quick. I thought she was going to end it, but she kept seeing him. Not all the time, more like once a month."

"Did he ever harm or threaten her?"

"No, not that she ever said. She found out he liked cocaine and was self-centered. I think she wanted to end it, but I think she liked the benefits, if you know what I mean."

"Did her husband know?"

"I'm not sure. She said he was beginning to ask questions, but as far as I know he did not have any proof. She was dumb at first, nearly getting caught at a client's house. After that she got smart and only met him out of town, and always made sure she had an alibi."

"Was anything else bothering her? Angry client, other family problems, that kind of thing?"

"She was good at her job so I don't know that anybody was mad at her. Typical family stuff among her family and in-laws, but no trouble with them."

"I appreciate your time today. I don't plan to tell anyone what you told me. I will use what you've said to take a closer look at her boyfriend."

"Please keep me out of it anything to do with Tammy if

you can. Because our boys are close, and I know most of the people she knew."

"I understand."

"Oh, there was something else bothering her."

"Do you know what it was?"

"No, she didn't say anything directly. I knew she was working on some big deals, and maybe one of them wasn't going through. Nobody was mad or anything, just some paperwork issues or something."

"Do you know her real estate partner, Joe?"

"Yeah, I've known him forever. We all went to school together."

"What do you think about him?"

"I guess he's always been ambitious. Asking out girls that wouldn't give him the time of day, acting like a jock when he was always second string on the team, that kind of thing."

"Was he always nice to you and Tammy?"

Cindy did not answer for a second. She then took a sip of tea.

"He was always sweet, sometimes too much so. And he was persistent to the point that he got yelled at sometimes. But I've never seen him or heard of him getting rough with any of us."

"Do you still keep in contact with him?"

She hesitated again. "I see him around sometimes."

"But he and Tammy must have gotten along since they were partners."

"I think they did. She seemed to deal with him better than most. Maybe she thought of him a little bit like an obnoxious kid brother. But they made it work."

"I don't think I have any other questions. Thanks again Cindy. Take care."

"You're welcome. Please get the guy responsible."

"I plan to."

I saw Cindy out then went back to the booth. There was a lot to think about. I still didn't see a clear motive and suspect. Lottie sat across from me.

"Did you find out anything useful?" Lottie asked.

"Good background on Tammy and the boyfriend. But…"

"Not enough there to get anywhere."

"There is insufficient evidence to pinpoint a suspect. What is really lacking is a motive. Or rather, a motive strong enough for murder. I think her husband could have killed her if he found out about the affair and lost his mind for a moment. And her partner might be sleazy, yet she didn't think him violent. I also got a feeling Cindy might be close to the partner."

"The lack of evidence of violence would rule out Robert and a fit of rage."

"Possibly. Or maybe he's got a different side than I've seen. Both the boyfriend and the partner are still options, but not good ones unless something new comes out."

"What does that mean?"

"Something important is still missing. I need to figure out what it is and how to get it."

"What do you think that was about trouble at work?"

"No idea. But I need to take another look at her partner. If not a crime of passion, then maybe it's about money. If Cindy does have a relationship with Joe, she might not be telling me everything."

"From experience, money and sex cover most motives."

"I think so too. Thanks for getting Cindy to talk to me."

Back home in my office I printed a photograph. I needed it for my afternoon walk. On the outer loop I saw Millard in his usual spot on the porch.

"Ahoy Millard. Permission to come aboard."

"Stop your nautical nonsense. There have not been any naval people around in years."

"I remember Roosevelt was connected to the navy as were his friends. Some of them were even here."

"They were, but the last one I remember died in 1970."

"I guess that was another era. Anyhow, I have something to show you."

"I'll get my glasses just as soon as I find them."

"They are hanging around your neck."

"Of course they are. Where else would they be?"

"This is the truck that belongs to Tammy's husband. He was driving it when he came to the funeral. Take a look and tell me if it could be the one you saw at the lake."

"Nope, this is not what I saw at the lake."

"How do you know?"

"The bed. It is too short for what I saw."

"OK, then I can rule out Tammy's husband."

"Are you sure? Do you have a picture of the other truck?"

"What other truck? This is what he came to the funeral in, so I'm pretty sure it is his."

"I don't doubt it, but that's his town truck. You'll also need to get a picture of his work truck so I can take a peek."

"How do you know he has a work truck?"

"Bet you my library he does. A farm that big he might even have more than one. Retires his town truck to farm use at some point, then gets a new truck. The new one he drives to town."

"That makes sense. But does not make me happy. Not sure how I will get onto his place to get pictures."

"There is an easier way."

"Which is?"

"Courthouse has tax records. Personal property includes registered vehicles."

"Yeah, that would be easier."

"Still not sure you are smart enough to cut my grass. But it is only a push mower, so you can't hurt yourself too bad."

"Thanks for your confidence in me."

"I'm just glad I don't have a riding mower. Not sure I could afford the liability of you trying to operate that."

I checked the records that night. Robert had three pickup trucks registered in the county. Unfortunately, there was not enough detailed information to get the color or what size bed the other two trucks had. I could not think of a good way to go on his property and check out the trucks without getting shot for trespassing.

CHAPTER TWENTY-ONE

A couple of days ago, on Thursday I had called Emma's cousin to catch up. I was then invited to lunch at their house. I accepted because I had not much to do and it was the correct social response. Besides, I wanted to visit the Cove, just south of Woodbury, where they lived.

The Cove got its name from the oddly-shaped geography. It was not a cove at all in the sense the word was used in the mountains, describing a narrow valley, usually with a stream in the middle. Rather, the Cove was cone-shaped. Maybe early settlers meant to say cone, but it came out cove.

Most people looking at a map with terrain and elevation would immediately recognize it as a crater. I had seen a couple of geological studies that said it wasn't. They said the unusual shape was instead because of the Flint River flowing across Pine Mountain and somehow creating a nearly circular crater. Experts had often been wrong about other geological anomalies, perhaps this was another mis-categorized geological feature. The bottom of the crater was approximately three miles across, making the area much larger than the town limits of Woodbury. Steep ridges rose four hundred feet, sometimes nearly vertical from the flat bottom along the circular border. Because the area was encircled with high ridges, Georgia Tech had placed telescopes inside the crater since they were protected from both light and radio wave pollution. Only one road traversed the crater and it was called Cove Road.

Sam and Irene lived there, backed up on one of the ridges that was not so steep. Sam was Emma's first cousin. I had met them both a few times over the years at family events but didn't know them well. They had lived in the general area most of their lives. But only at the Cove for the past twenty years. They still weren't considered natives around Woodbury, but they were no longer newcomers. That told me I needed to be in Warm Springs for twenty years to no longer be a newcomer.

I parked in their driveway. Coming up from the main road was twisty as the gravel drive had to make the best of the elevation gain. The house must have good views. The trees were mostly stunted hardwoods common to the Pine Mountain ridge system, along with mixed pine species.

I got out as Sam and Irene came out the door to greet me. Irene gave me a half-hug and I shook hands with Sam. They were about my age and looked like ordinary people. Emma had once said they ran with an edgy crowd. But that time must have passed, and I doubted Hamilton County had many edgy people in it anyway.

"James, welcome to our house in the Cove," Sam said. "It has been a while. How have you been?"

"I'm doing well," I said.

"We were so sorry to hear about Emma," Irene said.

"Thank you."

"Come in and we will show you around. Have you been to the Cove before?"

"I've driven through a few times. I wanted to see how much it looked like a crater."

"It is odd, isn't it?" Irene asked. "We hear different stories, so I don't know which is true."

"Me neither. But it looks like you have a view from up here."

"It is seasonal but nice," Sam said. "Out front you can see the steep ridge on the other side of the cove. Out back you can see part of the Flint River Valley."

We went inside and took a quick tour of part of the house and basement. It was nice, and I noticed a large gun safe downstairs.

"Sam, you must be a hunter."

"Not really. I've given up those cold, dark mornings. But I have a nice arsenal for home defense."

"Are you expecting trouble up here? It looks pretty tame in the Cove."

"No, not around here. But we keep plenty of protection around because of the old days. Can't be too careful."

I didn't say anything but tried to give him a questioning look. It did not work.

"But enough about that," Sam said. "Do you still hunt?"

"I gave it up completely. It got so that I didn't like anything about it. Kind of like drinking beer."

"Oh, how so?"

"I used to drink beer when I was young because everyone else did and it was available and cheap. But I never like the taste. When I got older I just quit because I didn't see the point."

"I see. How long have you been sober?"

"It's not like that. I still drink a cider or cocktail sometimes. Just not beer."

"Huh, I don't think I could live a week without a couple of beers on the weekend."

"I know, I have friends that really like beer. I never did and there are lots of alternatives."

"Yes, there are. And a lot aren't even alcohol-based. You know, smokes and edibles."

"There seems to be a lot of that around. Have not tried it since college though. I never did like smoking either."

"Tried the edible forms yet?"

"I should backtrack a little. When Emma first got sick we were traveling up along the coast. Stopped at a store in Maine and picked up both smoke and edible versions since it is legal there. She didn't like either one. Even the cat didn't like the smoke."

"That's too bad. Just like everything, people have different tastes."

"That they do."

"How did you like them?"

"I'm indifferent. But if I was sick I could see the benefit."

"Speaking of different tastes, let's go upstairs. Irene

should have lunch ready. By the way, if you ever need medicinals of any kind, just ask."

"Thanks."

Upstairs we had a nice lunch that was purely southern. Fried chicken, mashed potatoes, and pink-eye purple hull peas. It was great to have those staples cooked at home. It more than made up for missing brunch at Mable's. We caught up on the family that we knew in common. Then they wanted to know about the move down to Warm Springs and how the house was going.

"It has been good for me to work on the house and guest cottage," I said. "They are slowly looking better, not that the house needed a lot. But the cottage was eaten with termites, so it needs a lot of rebuilding."

"I hate termites," Sam said. "Our last house was treated but they got in the barn and nearly ate it all."

"They do make a mess."

"How do you like living on the Roosevelt campus?" Irene asked.

"I love it. I can walk to a lot of places I need, plus lots of general walking and hiking up on Pine Mountain."

"Sam and I drove past it a few years ago. Even then, we did not really notice what it was. It's been there all these years and nobody knows about it. We didn't even know it was there for all the years before that. It really is tucked away."

"It is, and not advertised. I've met people from Warm Springs that have not been there."

"James, we heard there was some trouble over there," Sam said. "A woman from Pine Mountain was found dead."

"It's true. It was quite a shock when I found her. Not something I was expecting on campus."

"You found her?" Irene asked. "That must have been terrible."

"I never got close, so it was not too bad. While walking I found her clothes by the lake and then further out I thought I saw a body. I called the police and they handled it."

"The paper said the poor woman must have been swimming and drowned," Sam said.

"That was the official story according to the state police. They didn't bother to do much investigating."

"You sound like maybe it was not an accident," Sam said.

"Oh no, it was not an accident, she was murdered."

Sam did not say anything but did not look surprised. Irene's mouth was open and her hand covered it.

"James are you sure?" Irene finally asked.

"I'm convinced but the police are not likely to reopen the case."

"Sounds like them," Sam said. "They make up their minds then write the reports to shore up their opinion. Police decide the first hour who is guilty or innocent, regardless of facts."

"It wasn't quite that bad in this instance. But they overlooked some things and didn't want the family to suffer any more."

"Do you really buy that?" Sam asked.

"No, I don't. Maybe a little about protecting the family. But it is more about protecting the political and business interests of the area. Murder is bad for them."

"You are right about that. So, is it over or what are you going to do?"

"I'm still investigating. Once I have enough evidence to convince myself I'll go after the murderer."

"There you go, take care of it yourself. Don't leave it to the folks you already know won't do anything."

"What does that mean James?" Irene asked. "Go after the murderer with a gun?"

"I hope not. I hope I'll soon have a plan, so I won't have to do that."

"Well, you be careful. People like that are the worst kind."

"To change the subject, I'd like you both to come over and see the house. I'll cook something up or we can go out if there's somewhere over there you want to go eat."

"Thanks James," Irene said. "Maybe next week."

"That won't work, Irene. We've got that business trip coming up. We'll be gone until the end of the month."

"Oh, that's right, I forgot."

"Call me when you get back and we will do it."

"Thank you, we will."

We all walked around the backyard for a few moments to look at the garden. They had a large outbuilding but we didn't visit it. Irene went back in to get me a large portion of strawberry shortcake to take back. I was too stuffed to eat dessert anytime soon.

"James, when you get around to going after the murderer, and I'm assuming it's a man, let me know."

"Why's that?"

"I got a lot of things that would persuade him to give himself up peacefully. Or if not, to take care of business."

"Are you talking guns?"

"Guns, grenades, a few other things. Whatever you think you might need."

"Thanks Sam. I still have several things I kept after my hunting days. I should be good."

"I thought so, but offering it if you need it."

"I appreciate it. But if he takes me out feel free to reciprocate." I said it as a joke but I wasn't sure that Sam noticed. He just nodded somberly.

We all said our goodbyes and I left. I drove around the Cove before going home. I still thought the place felt like a crater despite the expert's opinion. A very green crater blasted out of Pine Mountain. Or had the impact created the geological upheaval that created Pine Mountain? That was above my scientific pay grade so somebody else could figure it out.

Driving home, I was glad I had called and gone to see them. They seemed like nice people. Of course, Sam kept an arsenal for some reason related to security, had offered me plenty of light drugs, and offered to provide armed assistance. Who even had access to grenades? They were also retired but had a two-week business trip coming up. Maybe Emma was right, and they did have an interesting past. But I had enough of a mystery to piece together in Warm Springs.

I went home and worked on my meal preparation for the following week. Although I had been busy enough and driving out of town that some of last week's meals were in the freezer. At this rate I would soon be able to skip a week and forage from the freezer. Yet I somehow found the time and energy to eat the strawberry shortcake.

CHAPTER TWENTY-TWO

On my walk around the outer loop Sunday morning I heard a vehicle coming up behind me. I turned to see who it was before they got close just in case. Not long ago I would have not even thought about it. Rolling up behind me was a campus police SUV. I was not surprised when it slowly pulled beside me with the window down on the passenger side. We were on a deserted stretch of the road, out of sight and hearing of anyone for hundreds of yards. I doubted it was an accident that we were meeting here.

"Hi James."

"Hey Bryan."

"I should say something obvious like fancy meeting you here, or lucky I caught you on your walk."

"You could, but it isn't necessary. You must have a real situation developing."

"You might say that. Something came up. If you were interested in listening, I wanted to tell you about it. Get your logical opinion, unofficially of course. And I'd ask you not to repeat it."

"That is asking a lot when I don't know what it is going to be. If it ends up being a clue to a suspect I might have to follow it."

"I don't think that it will be that kind of a situation. But who knows, there have been a lot of curveballs thrown lately. So what do you think?"

"Let me try a different tactic. Do at least four other people know about what you want to discuss?"

"More like a dozen people."

"OK, then this gets easy. You tell me and I promise not to do anything stupid and never let anyone know you told me, regardless of what I do or don't do."

Bryan sat for moment, working the possibilities through his head. He turned off the car, took off the radio he wore, and got out. Those actions told me he was good with my promise. We went to the back of the car and leaned on the back hatch.

"There was a call earlier. Based on that call, Tammy's phone was found in the back of a pickup truck."

"If that is all there was, we would not need to have this conversation."

"That is the problem, it is complicated… Let me tell you the rest before biasing it with my opinion."

"Go ahead."

"An anonymous caller said there was a phone and case

matching Tammy's in the back of a large silver pickup truck. The truck was parked in the lot at the grocery store in Pine Mountain. A patrol car was a block away and drove over. Since it was in a public lot and in clear view in the bed, the officer picked the phone and flipped open the case. He saw Tammy's business cards in the phone case. The color of the case matched the one reported missing. The officer called it in and the chief there asked him to stay with it while he drove over. Their office is maybe five blocks away. He got there before the owner of the truck came out of the store with groceries and two kids. But when the owner did arrive it got a little heated, but the truck and phone were taken in so the state police could look at it. The owner was taken for questioning but not arrested after a relative picked up the kids."

"The truck owner was Robert, correct?"

"Yes."

"Was anything found on the phone?"

"Battery and sim card both missing."

"Were any fingerprints found on the phone or case?"

"No."

"Figures."

"What do you think this means?"

"Simplest explanation is that Robert did it and is the biggest idiot in the county. And it's a county full of good Samaritans that all have a description of the missing phone. One of those saints called it in."

"Isn't the simplest explanation usually the right one? Occam's razor?"

"Only for simple people. The right explanation is the correct one, regardless of how complicated it is."

"Well, there are some police right now thinking Robert did it."

"And they may not be wrong. The right answer has not been determined yet."

"What do you think is a more likely answer?"

"The killer dumped the phone in Robert's truck and called the cops."

"That makes much more sense than the first answer."

"And it is the same one you had already picked as right."

"Yeah, as someone who's chased both smart and dumb criminals, it makes sense to me. Robert's not that dumb, and somebody else is trying to be smart."

"It is nonsensical for Robert to pull the phone case off, rip out the sim card and battery, put it back together, leave Tammy's cards in the case, wipe off his fingerprints and nonchalantly toss it in back of his truck for anyone to see. I suppose there are no cameras outside the grocery store?"

"Already checked, and no there are not."

"Would have been too easy. This guy is camera shy."

"He's been clever so far."

"Did Robert say anything?"

"Other than some cursing, no he didn't. Soon as he got to the station he refused to talk and got his lawyer."

"Smartest thing he could have done."

"He's not dumb. Makes the whole thing look even more staged."

"Could he be that smart? Stage the stage so he gets a get out of jail free card because the police harassed him?"

"Possibly, but it doesn't fit his character. But who knows, maybe his lawyer put him up to it."

"You know his lawyer?"

"Yes, and yes he could have put Robert up to it."

"Wow, if I ever get arrested down here give me his name. I like the way he thinks. If he hasn't lost his license by then."

"You said 'if I ever get arrested down here' rather than just 'if I ever get arrested.' Makes me think you've been in trouble before."

"We both know anyone can get arrested for almost anything. I've never been caught for anything."

"That's not exactly making me feel better."

"I hope not. But I only work for the good guys now."

"Guilty conscience?"

"Every day, Bryan, every day."

"Is that why you are good at chasing bad guys?"

"A hundred percent. Problem is, everybody is bad at some level. So, there is a lot of sifting to find the right bad one. Tell me I'm wrong."

"You are not, because that is what we spend most of our time doing. Except for the lazy ones of us that choose to blame the first bad one they come across."

"Yeah, it's justice, it's just not right."

"Does it make sense to you for somebody to do this since the case is closed?"

"Not really. It's a slight risk, because if the case reopens to look at Robert, something might show up that leads back to the perpetrator. No reason to do that unless he's feeling pressure."

"I think he is feeling pressure."

"From where?"

"I'd say he's heard there is a nosy fellow from Warm Springs going around and asking questions."

"Are you serious?"

"I don't know of any other reason. You have somebody worried. Do you have a gun?"

"Of course I do. Are you saying I need it?"

"My professional opinion is yes. I smell the slight scent of desperation in the air."

"I appreciate the warning."

"Hope the rest of your day goes better than talking to me. You've got the picnic today for the garden volunteers, don't you?"

"Yes, we are getting together. Should be fun."

"Alright, I'm on my way. I have bank robbers and old men on scooters to chase."

My walk home was a little more exciting than expected. I needed to put out one of my pistols in easy reach somewhere in the house. Then I forgot about it at home as I needed to get food together.

Our garden group was having the first picnic this afternoon. I had volunteered to do the food. George was bringing the iced tea and dessert. We would try it once a month and rotate who brought food and drinks.

I had been thinking about the food. For a safe picnic, items needed little or no refrigeration. Also, everything needed to be easy to eat by hand, so nothing sticky or gooey. That would keep down the fire ant and fly pests as well. It was hard to eat a casserole or salad without utensils, so those were off the menu. I needed to make things similar to what was available at the county fair to walk around with, but healthier. It was not going to be easy.

After a lot of dead-end thoughts, I came up with sausage balls with extra cheese, ham sandwiches, and corn on the cob. The sandwiches would be bread from Mable's, the ham I'd just made, and spicy mustard with a touch of steak sauce. I used mayonnaise at home but not for picnics or anytime food would be left at room temperature. Otherwise it was dysentery broth. I considered using a puree of avocado but ruled against it. Could still be messy and green stuff on ham reminded me of Dr. Seuss. The corn I found at the farmer's market. It must have been imported since it was a few months too early for local. But it was fresh and sweet, needing no butter. Just a sprinkle of coarse sea salt to make it great. It roasted nicely. The sausage ball biscuits I made for Ison were still on my mind, but I didn't need them large since I was serving sandwiches. Maybe I could make them more in the shape of cheese straws or "fries" to have a unique shape and more surface area to get crispy. Or I could roll them flat before baking like chips. I tried both. The fries were the winners.

I put everything on my bike since it was basically a cargo carrier. We were gathering in the actual quad behind the Georgia Hall, on tables under the trees. George, Edna, Wes, Ernie were already there with iced tea poured. I unloaded the food on the table. I got some unusual looks. "OK, I know this is not traditional picnic food, but give it a try."

Everyone began eating and the grumbling died down.

"I thought you were crazy when I first saw this," Edna said. "Now I get it. Don't need to keep it refrigerated and it is easy to eat. You put the cheese in the sausage balls rather than on the ham sandwich. But somehow it all works together. And the corn is real nice."

"Thanks. That was the general idea. My food ideas don't always work out, but it did this time."

Twenty minutes later the food was gone, and it was time for dessert. George brought up a large metal canister from a cooler. It was homemade peach ice cream. It violated all my picnic rules, but it was excellent just the same. The second bowl was nice as well.

Clean up was minor and we talked a few minutes about plans for the next garden session. All the seeds and starts were in, so we were about to begin planting in earnest. But first the drip irrigation system had to be set up. As we broke up to leave, George walked with me.

CHAPTER TWENTY-THREE

"You know Alisha?" George asked.

"I don't think so."

"She is at the information desk at the hospital. Where you check in."

"Oh, I've seen her then. I don't remember talking to her though. Why?"

"She's been taking some time off. The ladies over at the hospital are talking."

"George, where are you going with this?"

"She's been off work because she's pregnant. First time and apparently, she has had some minor complications."

"That's too bad, I hope she's OK. I assume her husband or partner can look after her."

"He can't, not really. Since he's not officially in her life. Because he's married to someone else. Or was until recently."

"I still don't see why you're telling me."

"The father is Robert."

"Robert, as in Tammy's husband? Are you sure?"

"I didn't want to get into this. But the ladies at the hospital and the cafeteria all know, and they've made it known that I should tell you."

"Oh, I get it. You got picked to deliver this stinky diaper."

"Pretty much. But everybody knows you are working on this thing and you needed to know."

"Thank you, George. You can pass on my thanks to the others as well. Did they have any other information?"

"Not that I know about. But if they come across anything I'm sure I'll be telling you about it."

That was interesting. Apparently, Tammy wasn't the only one of the couple pursuing an extramarital tryst. Would that make him more of a suspect?

"George, if I could impose upon you, I'd like to send back a couple of questions to the group."

"Sure, go ahead."

"First, can you ask them how long they've been seeing each other. Second, was Robert ever mean to Alisha. Last, did Tammy know anything about it."

"I'll ask them. Might be a day or two for it to filter out to everybody."

"That's OK. Time is not pressing."

I needed time to think about the implications of

George's revelation. I went and sat on my front porch. Would Robert's affair have set off a series of problems where he thought the only solution was killing Tammy? She might not have even known about it, but the towns in the area were small enough that I was sure the baby's arrival would have gotten back to her. Certainly the campus staff knew already, and I imagine some of them might even live over in the town of Pine Mountain. Or, and this was something new I had not considered, was Alisha capable of murder? Maybe she and Robert were acting together as a murder team? Alisha could have lured Tammy over to campus and drugged her. Then Robert put her in one of his trucks, drove to the lake, and put her in the water.

Interesting. Not long after I talked to Cindy, two incriminating stories came up about Robert. Was it coincidence, or karma if Robert was the killer? Or was it someone trying to make Robert look guilty?

On Monday morning, inside the large foyer at the hospital, I took a chair where I could see the check-in desk. The attractive and dark-haired girl I vaguely remembered was sitting there on the phone. I went to the gift shop nearby and perused some things I had no intention of buying while watching Alisha. She got up and retrieved a folder from the other side of the counter that was wide enough for three people to work behind. I suppose budget cuts or lack of patients had resulted in fewer staff.

I observed two things about Alisha. She was not showing her pregnancy and she was maybe five feet tall and ninety pounds. The timing of her pregnancy was interesting, as I guessed she could not have been more than four or five months along. Cindy said Robert was suspicious about Tammy the past few months. Perhaps he was talking to Alisha about his problems and things went further than talk. There was no way of knowing without asking her or Robert directly, and I had no intention of asking either one.

Alisha's stature told me something else. No way did she haul Tammy's drugged or dead body anywhere. Not even with a wheelbarrow. Especially if she was already having pregnancy issues. But it did not rule her out completely, as she could have still helped Robert do it. Somebody close to Tammy had to have been involved or there would have been a struggle.

I decided to switch tactics. It was time to meet Robert. On the walk home, I stopped to see Bryan at his office.

"Hi James."

"Hi Bryan."

"What can I do for you?"

"Just a couple of questions about Tammy's husband, Robert."

"I'll tell you what I can."

"What do you know about him?"

"I know him from a committee we were on together a while back. He's not a shirker. He inherited a lot, but he still works hard."

"Does he have a temper?"

"I know he used to. I asked one of my guys about him after we met. He remembered going to a high school football game, the big rivalry with the next county over. He said Robert started a fight during the game. Word was they got into it again after the game was over at a convenience store on the county line. Police broke it up and didn't arrest anyone."

"I need to meet Robert but I'm not sure how to do it. I'd like to get a better idea of who he is."

"You could try going to the kid's baseball games. Although I'm not sure they are still doing that. He may have taken them out of the league this season after all that's happened."

"That might not be the best setting. It is also unlikely I'll happen to run into him in town sometime unless I stalk him. Besides, trading a few words at the grocery store won't get me what I need."

"You might try his store."

"What store?"

"The agricultural supply store in Manchester."

"I thought somebody else owned it. I heard Robert was in some sort of agriculture business, but I figured he was selling cattle or hay."

"He bought it a few years ago after the owner retired. Kept the name so not many people know he owns it."

"Does he work there?"

"He has a manager, but I think he's there a couple of times a week. Look for his truck."

"If he drives to Manchester then he goes right by here on the way."

"Or takes the ridge road. But yeah, he probably comes right in front of campus. Where Tammy's car was found."

"Robert's potential suspect value keeps increasing."

"You should pay him a visit."

Manchester was just four miles from Warm Springs. A larger town, it was centered on a railyard and owed its early growth to a cotton mill. It had schools in town and fast food restaurants. Chain restaurants passed for royalty in the region. Otherwise you had to travel quite a distance to get a mediocre burger once hawked by a clown.

Overall it was a grainy place, rundown in that old tired southern town way. The mill had closed and since burned. A nice house stood by one that was abandoned, and down the street was a place that should have been abandoned for the good of everyone. Watching it from afar, I wondered how the town would progress.

It did have a public library, a small grocery, and a couple of local restaurants. Because of its size, location, and infrastructure, it seemed ripe for revitalization. I hoped someone would get to it soon.

Entering the parking lot of the agricultural supply store, I wondered how the conversation with Robert would go. I did not need any farm supplies, so I would have to wing it. Inside the store, I quickly realized it was geared to the needs of animal owners. No farm equipment, tools, or pallets of feed. The shelves held horse care products, from hoof kits to blankets, goat dewormer, feed supplements, bird feeders, and even a large section for dogs and cats. I didn't have to concoct a story after all.

There was one guy up front and I saw Robert in the back. The first guy asked if I needed any help. I told him it was my first time in the store and I would look around first. I did, and slowly worked my way toward the back.

"Do you sell antibiotics like amoxycillin, in case my cat needs it?" I asked Robert.

"We can do that if you have a prescription from a veterinarian."

"Oh, so it is not like the old days when I got it over the counter."

"That's right. The regulations changed, so it has to be by prescription."

"Do you carry everything a vet can prescribe?"

"Most antibiotics, supplements, and hormones but not drugs. You have to get those direct from the vet."

"Got it. My cat is accident-prone so she is at the vet a couple of times a year." I didn't think Kat would mind me stretching the truth a bit. She was about as healthy as a cat could get.

"Some cats are like that. She a barn cat?"

"No, she's an outside cat but more domestic. Gets to stay inside at night after a good meal."

"With the coyotes and other predators around here, it is smart to keep her inside."

"I don't think I have too much to worry about. I live on the Roosevelt campus in Warm Springs. You know where that is?" I had ambushed him and waited for a reaction. What I saw was him hesitate, his face draw up like he'd just seen a bad accident, and maybe his eyes even teared up a little. His voice was tight when he answered.

"I do. Well, if you have any prescriptions you need to fill, come see us. Take a look at our cat section to see if she needs something else." He turned and walked off.

"Thanks, I will," I said to his back. I looked some more and bought a couple of things. In my car on the way back to Warm Springs I replayed my encounter with Robert. I did not get any red flags. Still, I wondered about his access to ketamine through the store. They might not stock it, but he must have contacts in the industry. Yet his reaction seemed genuine and sad when I mentioned the campus. My gut was still not convinced he was the killer. I needed more evidence to push on all three suspects.

CHAPTER TWENTY-FOUR

I felt I had a decent profile for the husband, Robert, and could develop one for the partner Joe. Both were local so I could continue working on them, passively on Robert but actively for Joe. I was not getting any closer to developing all the background on the boyfriend. Larson Bristow was not going to be easy to develop as a suspect because I didn't have the background or the official designation to investigate him properly. But I knew people that could do it. The price was high as I had to talk to them.

I stopped at a large retailer and picked up a prepaid phone. I called a number I knew by heart but called less than once a decade. It was a working payphone in a business in Atlanta. How many payphones still existed? But this one did and for a reason. A random person answered. I left my name and number for a particular person. When they got a burner phone they would call back.

I waited for the someone from a past life that was probably best forgotten. He likely felt the same. Or maybe not, as he had always called back and seemed to keep up with me. But this situation superseded my feeling for him. As one of the youngest members of the old Dixie Mafia, he was probably one of the last original members. Not that they had a member list and reunions, as it had never been a tight organization. Yet they did have an extensive if dilute network.

The Atlanta group was one of the more resilient branches. They had not died out but had changed forms and membership several times over the years. Other groups had disintegrated after killing each other off or been decimated by federal law enforcement. The Atlanta chapter survived by moving away from hard drugs since that drew too much attention from law enforcement or vicious drug gangs. They fell back on softer if less lucrative pursuits of gambling, prostitution, and theft. Car theft and chop shops around northern Georgia was their specialty. For the right price they would do other things.

An hour later I got a call back on my new phone. Afterwards I'd rip it apart and dispose of it. We didn't spend any time on catching up. I gave him three names with addresses. Just under sixty seconds later we were done. Even with burner phones brevity was safer. I would wait two or three days, get another phone, and call back the payphone. That would be the prelude to a longer conversation, so I would get an appointment to discuss in person.

Three days later I got an invite in the convoluted way

we always did. My destination was a MARTA subway station near the Atlanta airport. It was so he could not easily be followed should the FBI be interested in his travels, and no auditory equipment to record him from a distance. I was OK with it, as it protected me as well. I was also coming in from a different direction. Our meeting would be held standing outside the station and under the flight path of the jets. Atlanta was so busy there were always jets to provide background noise. Ear-shattering, bone-jarring noise. I was not looking forward to it. I found him loitering near the entrance to the parking garage. He motioned for us to go in the garage, where we took the elevator to the top of the garage, under the sun and screaming jets.

"You haven't changed much," he said. "Just older."

"It's a habit I hope to hold on to a little longer."

"We all hope to. Don't mean it'll happen. The guys said hello."

"I didn't know any were left."

"Two are gone, cancer and heart attack. Art and Benjy."

"Sorry to hear that."

"It's OK. I know you don't do homecomings and holidays. Let's get to business."

"Sure."

"The first guy, the one called Larson. He moves and slips around but never quite crosses the line into real trouble. You know these Harley riders that run around on their motorcycles acting tough in little towns? The ones that are actually dentists and chiropractors with the silly rebellious goatees?"

"Yeah, unfortunately I know that species."

"That's him but younger. He'll probably get a Harley when he gets older. Right now, he drives a Hummer and snorts coke on the weekends for fun."

"You see him killing anybody?"

"Only if he runs over them when he's drunk in the Hummer."

"Not violent or drug addled?"

"Has not been to date. If you want, we could shake him a little, see what falls out of his pockets. Sometimes it takes a little coercion to get to a man's true nature."

"Not necessary. Does he have any major debt?"

"Spends more than he makes most months. Get this, he's also a trust fund baby. Grandfather made it big in chickens up in north Georgia. So, his spending doesn't get him in trouble or tied up in our loan business."

"OK, not violent and not in money trouble. Unless he is just a murderer he probably didn't kill his part-time girlfriend."

"That is what this is about. Should have told me, I could have checked his rep further on that end. Killing ladies takes a special kind of wacko. Although what we saw was that he gets plenty of opportunities with his gym clientele. No hookers that we could confirm."

"OK."

"Now as for being a murderer, he could be. I know guys that like killing just to kill. Or he could have been in a steroid rage. He buys that stuff too. Give me another week and I'll see what is buried in his basement."

"This other guy, Joe, get anything on him?"

"Not much on the murder side, but what I know is

interesting. Small towner with an attitude, always thinks he's right."

"How so?"

"One of those idiots that got big into fantasy football."

"Nothing wrong with that."

"No, but he got all full of himself. Then along came legalized gambling."

"I don't see that being a problem either."

"It's not, exactly. Except when you lose as much as he has, it makes you do things to cover the big losses. Like bet even more, then lose even more."

"How deep in is he?"

"Four hundred thousand as of last month. Probably more now. He is in deep to some bad people. His biggest mistake was taking money from us in Atlanta, then sneaking over to New Orleans to get more money. Guess he didn't figure we would compare notes anymore. He was wrong. About twenty percent of our clients try that move."

"Are these the kind of people that might kill his business partner to make a statement?"

"No, it's not like the old days. But he is at the point now where he's due a roughing up and sending some guys to take whatever he owns that they can grab. After that if he doesn't work out payment then we will bury him with lawyers. Hasn't happened yet because New Orleans and Atlanta are still working out who will do it. Most likely will be us, to save on travel expenses."

"Lawyers? A kinder, gentler mob these days?"

"Something like that. More efficient. He will get roughed up to a point. But killing is bad for business.

Lawyers are good for business. And nothing is more important than the business making money."

"Anything on violence or women?"

"Nothing on that end. He's used an escort service in Atlanta that we have part ownership in. Has fetishes but no violence with the girls."

"Lastly, hear anything about the husband, Robert?"

"I don't know him, and nobody up here knows him. Seems to have family money and property. If he's into something it's outside our jurisdiction."

"No gambling, stolen property, or hookers?"

"Nope. We checked with Birmingham, New Orleans, and Florida. He's clean as far as we know, or awfully careful."

"OK, thanks for that. What do I owe you?"

"Nothing, because I didn't do anything. Just talking."

"I appreciate it."

"Heard about Emma. Real shame about that."

"Thanks."

"Last time I saw her was at your wedding. But I knew she was a good one."

"I have to go before traffic gets bad."

Driving back, I thought about my distant past. I had a few family members I was not proud of once I got older. But when I was young, I didn't know any better and thought all families had some edgy characters. I also did some things as a teenager I was not proud of when associating with them.

I got my act together and escaped to college. My sense of self-preservation kicked in because I knew most criminals got caught. I never went back to Atlanta to live or even visit those relatives. But maybe once a decade I ran into them or saw somebody at a funeral. Funny how I almost ended up with that crew. A few of them were full-time criminals, some part time, and one was a dirty cop working the inside.

I had to admit I learned from them about how the world really worked on different levels. Sometimes that came in handy. I also learned it wasn't how I wanted to live my life, so maybe they were role models, in a sense.

Another few years and they would all be gone. None of their children opted to continue that line of work. Somebody else would take their place, probably younger and meaner. It would not be my concern. I once thought to turn in all the people I knew to make the world a better place. Then I realized that big business the world over was just a refined version of what some of my family did in Atlanta. People liked their vices and were willing to pay for it regardless of the cost.

What had I learned today to further my investigation? Nothing useful on the husband. I was hoping for more on Larson the boyfriend. He seemed a playboy without any known violence or money problems. Joe the partner was a weasel when it came to money and had a gambling addiction. To the point that he was likely desperate. But no obvious violent tendencies. I needed more information on all three to find a motive worthy of murder. But I decided to concentrate on the local guy with the most to lose first.

CHAPTER TWENTY-FIVE

I called Joe Burgess, Tammy's business partner and co-broker at their realty office in Pine Mountain. I told the receptionist who answered that I'd like to speak to the broker in charge to list a house. Five seconds later he was on the phone. The promise of a listing got his attention. Most realtors were decent, but the worst realtors nearly piddled themselves to get an easy listing, so that already told me something about Joe.

My story, after a brief introduction, was that I had bought the house in Warm Springs, but because of family issues I needed to sell. When I told him where it was I caught a slight hesitation in his response. But he quickly warmed back up. It was too good a property in a great location to let a little thing like a dead body found nearby mess up a sure thing. I thought it interesting he did not mention that his partner died a few hundred yards away just days ago. He said he'd come to my house in an hour for a quick walk through. We would work out the listing details after that.

Upstairs, I put the whiteboards into the attic storage. I didn't want one of the suspects to see his name displayed in my murder matrix. For a moment I thought about leaving them out just to see Joe's expression but decided against it.

I sat on the front porch to await him. He arrived in a big, almost new truck. One of those with the wide side mirrors although I doubted he had ever towed anything with it. Four doors and a long bed. Probably had an elevator to help him get in it. I knew it cost considerably more than my first house purchase. But he was a realtor, so it was probably a business write off.

I showed him the inside of the house first. As soon as he came in, Kat took one look at him and took off upstairs. After seeing the house we walked around outside to see the lot. He didn't seem to care about the guest cottage, so we did not go in. I told him it would have to be sold in an as-is condition because I would not be finishing it soon. I had decided to go back to Asheville, so I wanted to sell quickly. He didn't think it was going to be a problem. I could see the cash register in his head ringing up his profit for minimal work.

We went out front to where he was parked. "James, I believe we can sell this house in a few days once it is listed. Are you going to be ready to move that quickly?"

"Yeah, I think so. I'm ready to get back to old friends

and away from the summer heat. Do I need to do anything to get it ready?"

"No, everything looks good. I saw you have a cat so the showing agent will need to know about it. Does it need to stay inside?"

"That should not be a problem. I'll take her with me when the house gets shown."

"Great, that will help. Once we get the listing ready I'll be back to put a lockbox on the front door."

"No need. The code to the front door is 9001. You can use it to get in when I'm not here or for a showing."

"Thanks, but it will be best to have a lockbox. Agents from other offices will expect it."

"OK, that works too. Joe, that is a good-looking truck. I'm thinking of buying one like it since I'll need one in the mountains."

"It is a nice one. I love it. Drives great and has not been any trouble since I've had it."

I walked around and looked at the exterior. "Mind if I look at the bed and inside the truck?"

"No, go ahead."

I opened the tailgate and looked in the truck bed. There were no scratches or dents. I doubt it had ever been used for much of anything. There was a wheelbarrow in it, the kind most people have with one wheel up front. It was upside down and held in place by rubber straps. It looked new.

"I think the bed is big enough to put lumber and sheetrock in. I've got some building to do."

"I believe it is. I've seen contractors around here with

the same model truck, full of supplies in the back. Even ladders."

I opened the rear door behind the driver's door. I could have looked in, but the truck was quite tall and the side windows were tinted too dark.

"Wow, that is a big seat and lots of leg room."

"It is roomy back there. I have not needed it, but I could probably get three adults or five kids in there."

"I believe it." I closed the door and went up to the hood where Joe was standing.

"I'm impressed with your truck and I have a favor to ask. But I'll understand if you don't want to."

"Sure, go ahead and ask."

"Can you drive me around the outer circle once, just so I can get a feel for how it rides? It won't take but five minutes."

"Sure, hop in. I think you'll like it." While I was going around to the passenger door, I pulled out my phone and sent a quick text before getting in.

"Sorry, I had to let my physical therapist know I would be a few minutes late."

"Oh, something wrong?"

"Not really, or rather, nothing new. Working on my knees so I won't have to get surgery. One of the perks of getting old."

Joe drove away from the house and turned on the outer circle. He yammered on and on about sound systems and navigation and collision avoidance. I had no idea what he was saying. I didn't care since I'd never buy a monstrosity like this. As we passed Millard's house I saw him standing on the porch watching us go by. I didn't wave. Even if I had, he would not have seen it through the window tint.

As Joe made the last turn before getting on the road to my house, I heard something rolling around in the floorboard behind my seat. It sounded heavier than a drink bottle. Joe pulled into my drive.

"Thanks Joe, I really appreciate the ride. It's a nice truck."

"It is, and I think you'd be happy with it."

"Oh, before you go, I wanted to climb in back to see just how big it is. I do have a lot of extended family I might have to cart around when I get back to Asheville."

"Go ahead."

I hopped down then climbed in the back. The object rolling around was a silver gas canister, about quart sized, with a breathing mask. I pushed it under the seat with my foot, rolling it over to see if there was a label.

"Don't mind the junk back there. Somebody probably left a drink."

"No problem, I don't see anything. This really is a big space back here. Perfect for what I need. Thanks again for showing me your truck."

"Glad you like it. I'll be in touch in a couple of days to get the listing started, and let you know what day it goes active. I'll send the contract and disclosures by email. Please sign and send back so I can finalize the listing."

"No problem, and thanks again."

Joe left. I was rid of him and his truck, and despite having to put up with him I was a little further along the way to establishing a working hypothesis for Tammy's murder. Since I didn't have a good motive or suspect, and I was not a criminal justice major, I would apply scientific methods and create a hypothesis with what I did know. It sounded so professional but really, I was just making stuff up that could be right. I went inside to go write on my white board upstairs.

Later I walked the outer loop. As I expected, Millard was on his porch.

"Took you long enough to come around."

"I had some notes to make. My mind isn't as sharp as it used to be."

"Just you wait. Soon enough you'll be writing reminders on the toilet paper to zip up your pants."

"Nah, by then I won't be wearing pants. Isn't there a nudist colony for the elderly? Clothing optional assisted living."

"If there is such a place I expect you'd find it. You might want to lose your eyesight before you go, however."

"I appreciate the tip."

"You're probably wondering what I saw."

"It did occur to me."

"Well, can't say it is one hundred percent, but I'm sure that was the type of truck I saw at the lake the night Tammy died. Big, four doors, right bed length. Color might be the same too, but hard to tell at night."

"Thanks for eyeballing it for me."

"Good thing you texted when you did, I was about to go take a shower."

"Hope I didn't disturb you too much."

"You didn't."

"Say Millard, that looks like a pie tin that they have at Mable's."

"Really? Wonder how that got here."

"You old devil, that's why you needed a shower. You've been getting a special delivery."

"So that's what they call it nowadays. I was wondering about the latest slang terms."

"Don't take me there, Millard. The visual may prevent me from ever thinking about sex again. I was referring to the contents of the pie tin, that was all."

"Hah, a prude, I knew it. You would be embarrassed by some of the stories of the shenanigans that went on all over this campus."

"I've heard rumors."

"Those rumors were tamped way down. Nobody wants to hear about the disabled carrying on like regular people. Nor that the carrying on was way past what regular folks around here even imagined."

"I might want to sit down one day and talk about that. Not the details, but more about who the people were."

"You bring me a couple of those pies and plan to be here all day. I'll make coffee and fill your brain with all sorts of things you would not believe."

"I don't know if those are the stories I'm looking for. Maybe you need to get out more."

"Wish I could."

"You plan to get the bum hip repaired someday?"

"I looked into it more than once. I would like to get out of the house and go about more."

"What is holding you back?"

"You know what the two worst outcomes are for an eighty-year-old patient going in for surgery?"

"I have a good idea but tell me."

"Hospital-acquired infections. You go in and don't ever come out. Pneumonia and sepsis aren't survivable at my age."

"I agree. What is the second one?"

"Stroke. Chances are good I'd have one during or within twenty-four hours of surgery. Bet you didn't know that."

"I did actually. A stroke got my eighty-six-year-old grandmother after a simple gall bladder surgery."

"See, it's a real problem."

"It is, even with all the new practices. Surely there is some solution."

"Maybe, but you'll never see me with a walker. I've tried using a cane but after a hundred yards it doesn't help any."

"Maybe you need a moped."

"Too old for two wheels. But I used to have a motorcycle. Now I just need a go-cart. But one high enough I can get in and out of."

"A lifted cart. Don't think I've seen one of those."

"Me neither, otherwise I'd get one."

"Well, take care. I'll see you in a few days to cut the jungle you call a yard."

CHAPTER TWENTY-SIX

I had a phone call to take after making a few gyrations of carousel phones. It was the follow up from my conversation at the subway station in Atlanta.

"Hello."

"We looked into Larson and whether he might be a killer. We didn't find or hear anything. If he does it, he keeps it random and quiet. Or, like I said before, he could have flipped out and did it the one time. But none of the girls around him report any violence."

"Thanks for looking into it."

"The other one we both know, Joe. His situation just got worse. He's about to experience some unpleasant days. Turns out his payment plan might have fallen through. He can't get his wife to bail him out."

"Does she have money?"

"Does pretty well. Being a dentist in Columbus pays for the house and keeps her separate account funded. But she's smart enough not to give him money. He'd probably just gamble it rather than pay his debts. They'd have lost the house if it wasn't in her name."

"Sounds like he's desperate."

"He doesn't know desperate yet, but he will next week."

"Thanks again."

"Good luck. Talk to you in another ten years if I'm still alive."

"Good luck to you too."

The last important clue had finally fallen into place. I went to see Bryan.

"Hey James. You are getting to be a regular."

"Sorry about that. Soon I hope you won't be seeing me."

"What do you need?"

"Bryan, if you can make it happen, it is important to do some more testing on Tammy's case."

"OK, what am I supposed to be looking for?"

"Nitrous oxide poisoning."

"That should have been covered by the toxicology screen."

"I bet it wasn't."

"Let me check." There was silence for two minutes while he scanned the report. "You are right, it was not tested."

"From what I know, nitrous oxide is not normally tested for in an autopsy. But I bet her lungs were full of it and that is why she was floating."

"The nitrous oxide made her float?"

"Not directly. But if she was dead from inhaling the nitrous before going into the water, her lungs would not have filled with water from drowning, so she floated. That is more believable than she was one of the two percent that die from dry drowning."

"OK, got it. How do you know so much about nitrous oxide?"

"It turns cooked meat pink."

"Uh, what?"

"Long story. It was a side project in my research days. But nitrous oxide can turn meat a pink color, makes it look raw even though it is cooked. A problem for the industry."

"Figures you would know that. I don't know what you did, but it must have been strange."

"Often was. But no time to reminisce. I just hope there is a lab in Georgia that can run the newest test procedures for nitrous oxide in tissue or blood. Say, would the original blood samples from the state lab still be held in storage?"

"I don't know but I can check. Supposed to hold thirty days unless the coroner or DA asks for longer for a suspicious death or homicide. But that might get Woods and Sims back in the loop."

"Hansel and Gretel? Can't be helped. They will know soon enough anyway."

"You are convinced it was a murder. Do you know who did it?"

"Not yet, but I'm betting on the top three usual suspects. My suspicion is based on motive and access, but I don't have enough information yet. But I think the weapon was nitrous oxide. This was not a random murder."

"Which of them has nitrous oxide?"

"Larson the boyfriend could have gotten it for illicit recreational use. Joe could have gotten it from his wife, the dentist. I have no idea about Robert."

"I'll request the test. It may take some time to get results."

"That is OK. I don't think the suspects are going anywhere."

I thought my day was about over. I wanted to have a bite and sit down with Kat for a while and rest my brain. There was a knock on the door. I wasn't expecting anyone. When I opened it I was quite surprised at who I saw.

"Mr. Wilder? I'm Alisha, can I talk to you?"

"Yes, come in Alisha. And call me James."

"Thank you." From her face and posture I could tell she was uncomfortable. Kat immediately came over to investigate. Alisha bent down to offer her hand which was accepted. She petted Kat as she rubbed against Alisha's leg.

"Alisha, would you like something to drink?"

"Oh, no thanks."

"Would you like to sit down at the table or outside?"

"The table is fine. What a wonderful cat." Kat had already performed a valuable duty. She obviously liked Alisha, who was already noticeably more comfortable. Kat followed her over to the table as we sat to continue receiving attention.

"Don't say that too loudly. You'll spoil the princess even worse. She likes you."

"I've always liked cats."

"Alisha, what can I do for you?"

"There have been a lot of rumors about me lately. I think you know what I'm talking about."

"The only thing I've heard is that you are pregnant."

She blushed. "That is the one. I've also heard a rumor about you. Then I saw you in the gift store the other day. You think Tammy was killed and are looking into it."

"That is true."

"I thought we should talk, because Tammy's husband Robert is the father of my baby. That makes him, and me, look bad after what happened to Tammy."

"I understand your concern. What can you tell me about you and Robert?"

"It's not as bad as it looks. I've known Robert most of my life. I was two grades behind him and Tammy. When she went off to college we dated. Then she came back and she married Robert, like I thought would happen."

"I guess you were disappointed."

"I was, but it was not like I didn't expect it. We all moved on. I stayed friends with Robert, but Tammy didn't want me around. Last fall Robert called me, and I knew something was wrong. He suspected Tammy was cheating on him, but he was in denial that she really was. I'd already heard about it but didn't tell him that."

"It seems you rekindled your old relationship."

"It just happened. I don't think either of us was expecting it. Then I got pregnant and Robert felt so guilty. But I decided I was going to have the baby. This is probably my only chance. Although I knew people would talk, I am determined to do it."

"Good for you."

"You really think that?"

"If you want a baby and are able to take care of it, then

sure. What other people think doesn't matter. But I imagine Tammy wasn't happy."

"She didn't know. But it was only a matter of time. These towns are too small for those kinds of secrets. Robert was trying to find a way to tell her when, you know, Tammy died."

"Was Robert planning to leave Tammy?"

"No, he was staying with her and the kids. I was OK with that because that is just better for everyone. I have family here to help me."

"You've shown a lot of courage. Both deciding to have the baby on your own, and by coming here to talk to me."

"It seemed like the right thing to do. I hope you don't think either Robert or I had anything to do with Tammy's death."

"I don't think so. Kat is an excellent judge of character. She approves of you."

"Thank you for listening to me."

"Thanks for coming by. Alisha, I'd like for you to consider something."

"What?"

"I know you are pregnant and need to take care of yourself. But please think about coming to work with us at the garden."

"That… is not what I was expecting you to say. I heard about what is happening with the garden and I'd like to help. But I didn't know if people wanted me around."

"We'd be happy to have you. You get to be outside and you'll get fresh food most of the year."

"That sounds nice, thank you for asking. I know George

and Wes and they have always been nice to me. So sure, I'll do it."

"Good. We'll meet at the garden next Thursday."

After Alisha left, I went upstairs to look at the whiteboards. The pieces were finally clicking together. Nitrous oxide instead of dry drowning. Significant money problems. Efforts to make Robert look guilty. I wasn't sure I needed to wait on the nitrous oxide test results before taking further action.

I felt I had done the best I could with what I had. I had no further leads to take on Tammy's murder. Three suspects. Two of them had motives probably strong enough to murder her. I would like to say that for all three, but I didn't have enough on Larson the boyfriend. The weapon was iffy, but I thought my instincts were good. Honestly, I was convinced nothing I had was enough to get the state police to reopen the investigation. But I was convinced which one was guilty. At least enough to get stupid and make something happen. It came down to my gut to make a choice.

I made the call. He seemed surprised once I cited the evidence to him. I phrased it such that he would think I was going to extort him for lots of money in exchange for not turning him in. Money was the only thing he valued; my threat to take it away was designed to elicit a strong response. I figured he would be threatened enough to come right over. I doubted he had any choice after what I told him, then demanded from him. If he had killed once and gotten away with it, he would try it again.

I had no intention of going along with his plans. I had a well-used pistol and I'd confront him when he showed up. Maybe get a confession from him. Or I could hide my gun at first and maybe he would go into the television-favorite talking villain routine. Then I'd pull out my gun and ruin his evening. I pulled up the recording app on my phone. I just needed to press it to record everything.

The slight problem with my plan was he was ten minutes early. He must have already been near my house when I called. The keypad activated, and the door opened. Easy enough for someone used to working with such things, especially since I had given him the code. He came in quickly with his gun in his hand. I was standing in the middle of the room, phone in hand, a few feet from the drawer I needed to reach. I was on the way but had not yet gotten my gun. This might not work out as I had thought.

"James, good evening. Perhaps you were not expecting me quite so quickly."

"You are certainly prompt."

"I was nearby trying to decide whether to pay you a visit. Your call was timely."

"Lucky me."

"You have been a real pain by keeping things stirred up about Tammy. You were about to ruin my big payday. She nearly did and found out the hard way. Now I can't let you get between me and what I deserve."

"She was about to shut down the land deal."

"She got a conscious at a bad time. Some others were worried as well. But in a few minutes, everything will be back on track."

"Some others?"

"No reason to get into that. I don't want to get overly chatty. Rather I just want to be done with this and get home. I sent the family away since I knew this had to happen soon."

"I would not want to inconvenience you. But won't your phone give away your locations?"

"My personal phone is on and at home. Gives me a little alibi. Should someone ever ask about my work phone, I'll have to say it was lost."

"That is convenient."

"There is no one else here I assume. You seem to repel people." He was looking around while trying to not get distracted. Despite him being an amateur I saw no way to get past him to my gun or get his away from him. He glanced over at my shelves. "I see you are a writer. Do you have any of your suspicions written down?"

"Of course not, you can trust me."

"I'll go upstairs and look through your study before I leave. Possibly take your laptop just in case."

"I know you have to wrap this up, but how did you get her to take the ketamine and the nitrous oxide?"

"I put the ketamine in her water bottle, the one she always carried around. The one nobody found because I threw it into the Flint River. Just enough to make her woozy. We had done the nitrous before on a lark one night. I thought it might make her more compliant to my wishes, but it didn't work. This time I thought she wouldn't fight it since she'd done it before and because the ketamine had kicked in." The entire time he was talking he kept glancing at the shelf.

The bottle, the one that kept my attention on many nights, was an expensive, rare whiskey. Pappy Van something or other that everybody seemed to know about and want. The only thing I knew was it was worth as much as a used car. Not that I cared for such things. I should have kept it out of sight so anyone that knew what it was would not be tempted to try it or steal it. If they did they would be in for quite a surprise and I'd find myself in trouble. But I kept it out where I could see it. I needed to know it was there. It kept me honest. It was always there as a temptation, yet each day it was not touched was another victory. A badge of success that I was still living, breathing, and moving forward. It kept me from doing something I shouldn't, in the strange way like how my cat kept me alive.

He slowly walked over to the shelf while he motioned with the gun for me to move back. To my consternation I was getting further away from my gun. He picked up the bottle and read the label.

"Quite something you have here. I noticed it the other day."

"It is for a special occasion."

"I see it has been opened but none is missing."

"True. I've never quite brought myself to drink it. A sniff was good enough. Not that long ago I swore to never drink whiskey again. Keeping it around both reminds me and tempts me."

He loosened the top and sniffed it. "Excellent. I believe I'll have a glass to celebrate my victory. If it is any consolation, you get to stay alive a few more minutes."

He poured a heavy shot into the nice crystal glass I kept beside the bottle. All the while never looking away for more than a second and the gun never wavered. "I've always wanted to try this but never could afford it. I will get a bottle once the land deal goes through."

"Don't forget to take the glass with you or wash and wipe it down if you leave it."

"That is very kind of you to remind me. I'll wipe it and put your prints on it afterwards. You know, you aren't a bad guy, other than slinking around and getting into people's business. I wish I didn't have to shoot you in the head, but it is my nature to be careful. Your apparent suicide is necessary to my freedom and financial success."

"I understand."

"I'm also drinking this because I want you to watch me take from you what you've denied yourself. Just a tiny punishment before the main event. Because of what you intended to take from me. I admit to being an ass in that regard. But in a lot of ways I'm really a nice guy. Cheers."

He lifted up the glass, half full of the light brown liquid, worth perhaps two thousand dollars, and took a large sip. He swallowed and smiled. "Oh my, that is even better than I imagined. I had no idea whiskey this smooth existed. You don't know what you've been missing."

I kind of did, but I didn't want to spoil his joy. He took

another large sip and savored it with his eyes half closed. But he kept the gun on me.

"James my man, I applaud your taste. I might even have to take this bottle with me."

"Please do, with my compliments."

His mouth quirked, and his eyebrows raised as he processed my response. A few seconds later his right arm began shaking uncontrollably. The pistol hit the floor as his hand spasmed. He looked at his hand as if to command it, but he'd lost all motor control in that limb. His left hand, holding the whisky glass, was fine. Then he dropped to the floor as his left leg collapsed. Once down, his face twisted as he bit back a scream. Parts of his body spasmed then slumped limp, while other parts clenched in bone-breaking muscle contractions.

The neurological effects were interesting. It was a first-hand view of a special poison acting upon the human body. I stepped close and knelt down so he could hear me. I needed to speak before his nervous system completely shut down.

"Joe, I bought the bottle when Emma died. I believed the time would come when I would enjoy a glass in my hope to join her. It seems your needs have superseded my own. Good job."

"You bast…" His mouth failed.

"Ditto."

More writhing from one arm, which settled quickly as pink foam gushed from his mouth. Then silence. There was no more movement as all nervous activity ceased within his body.

I took a few minutes to consider the irony. Plus, I

needed time to make some plans. If I acted quickly and carefully, then Warm Springs would be a better place. But first I needed to get up the spilled whiskey. I was grateful none had landed on the Persian rug. Kat might accidentally track through it, which would not do at all. Although she had darted off as soon as Joe had walked in the door. She always was an excellent judge of character.

I needed to get to Joe's house. I was betting the illegal things he was doing were better hidden at home than at the office. Previously he told me he had an office in his basement, and just now he said his family was gone. I lifted the keys from his pocket and decided to make a quick drive over to his place.

Joe was clever but not smart. It did not take me long to find a small lockbox of documents which the police didn't need, but which I did. Interesting things were inside which explained more about why Joe did what he did. For no other reason than money. Apparently, Tammy was in a position to kill the deal, leaving Joe hanging in front of the Atlanta and New Orleans criminal organizations. By killing her he could take his commission and pay them off and also take her commission as profit for himself.

Thirty minutes later, I was back home and calling the police. As for the time lag since Joe's death, I didn't think thirty minutes would matter much to any investigation. The piece of crap that killed Tammy and nearly me was still lying on my floor, so he didn't care either. I hoped this incident had not inconvenienced Kat.

CHAPTER TWENTY-EIGHT

A day later I watched from a distance as the police searched Joe's house. I drove over just to see if Woods and Sims were there. But I couldn't tell if they were or not.

I had spent the rest of the previous evening after calling the police, and the first part of this morning, giving a statement and answering questions. My bottle instigated a lot of interest once I told my story. At first, they thought I was a genius getting Joe to have that drink, but then I told them it wasn't even planned. I was planning to get my gun but got surprised instead. Him drinking the whisky was pure luck. That is when they realized the implication of what the bottle was really for. I probably would have been disbelieved, but I had the conversation recorded on my phone.

Then this morning Woods and Sims had shown up. Both were polite but unfriendly. They knew they had missed a killer once, and how close they had come to allowing said killer to commit another murder, namely mine. I did not hold it against them. They had done what they could with what they had, even though their effort was the bare minimum. They had other cases to deal with while I was retired and only had this one to work on. But I think professional pride prevented either of them saying thanks, or apologize, or take me on a ride-along. I should have baked them a nice loaf of banana bread. It would have been worth it to see whether they would eat it, given how recently there was a poisoned dead man on my floor.

Later, Bryan went with me to my house. He needed to collect the bottle for evidence since it was the cause of death. "My god, James, I've seen that bottle a dozen times," Bryan said. "I always wanted to ask you for a drink."

"For your own good, I would have declined your request."

"No kidding. I appreciate it. Why did you keep it around?"

"Have you ever lost someone you couldn't live without?"

The silence went on for nearly a minute. "No. No I have not. But I think I understand. Good thing the jerk decided to celebrate early."

"His loss is my gain." Using a glove, I picked up the bottle. "Bryan do you need the contents for any reason?

"Just a few drops we can test to confirm the poison."

I carried the bottle to the kitchen and poured almost all

of it down the drain. I put the stopper back in and handed it to Bryan, then rinsed out the sink.

"Why did you do that? We would have returned the bottle and contents."

"Perception versus reality. I once thought it would be a good way to finalize things if I ever got to that point. But after seeing up close what it does to the human body, I think I'll let nature take its course."

"Welcome back to the living. Hope you stay a while."

"I will, Chief."

Perhaps everything would work out in time. I would get the documents to Charles Fleming, the now retired former real estate broker in charge of the office that Tammy and Joe, her killer, had taken over. Tammy should get the credit and the commission of the real estate deal, although posthumously. At least her family would benefit. Although the land deal's completion was now uncertain at best.

Another set of documents I found at Joe's house was interesting and unexpected. A large study detailed the environmental effects of the massive development planned for the ridge. Joe and Tammy had commissioned it at the direction of the buyers, according to a letter in the packet. But they wanted to be hands off in case it came back negative, so they routed the money to Joe via bitcoin. The currency of the truly corrupt. A bad report was to be buried and never see the light of day.

The study clearly stated the planned development was unsuitable and unsustainable, and that both an endangered toad and a tortoise would be wiped out from the area. Joe had the only copy, so he had put it in his lockbox and apparently never told anyone as instructed. I suppose Tammy had a crisis of conscious and objected to the deal. I doubt it ever occurred to her he would kill her over it. But she didn't know about his debts to bad people.

I drove to Columbus and paid cash at a copy center to make three copies of the full report. I bought envelopes and stamps at the post office, then mailed each to an address I had looked up this morning. The Southern Environmental Law Center and two other organizations that had some success in stopping developments in Georgia because of environmental problems. Whether they could stop this one I did not know, but the report should at least hinder or cause it to be substantially reduced.

There was another batch of papers that I had not decided what to do with yet. I may not have to do anything because what I read might not even be legal. Joe was involved with a scheme on the Roosevelt campus. A number of the vacant cottages and their lots on the outer loop road were to be transferred to a different type of organization, something quasi-public and quasi-private, called the Cottage Preservation Foundation, or CPF. The cottages would be preserved by using state funds to repair and refurbish them, then sell them to the highest bidder. The CPF designated Joe as the preferred, and only, broker to handle the sales. A small board would govern the CPF, with Benjamin as the chair and in charge of the renovation funds. The small group would be well compensated by the state and receive bonuses based on the cottage sales.

Again, I wasn't even sure it was legal or whether the state had approved it. But I thought it an interesting exploitation scheme and explained Benjamin's behavior.

Another document showed a New Orleans corporation was interested in buying all the cottages and clearing them for a condominium development. Why would the state spend renovation costs on cottages to have them demolished? The answer seemed obvious; Benjamin would direct the funds for renovations but pocket them after reporting the cottages were renovated. But the cottages would not be renovated. However, the non-renovated cottages would be sold at prices reflecting renovations they didn't get to the New Orleans corporation. That would jump up Joe's commission and make the CPF a nice, false profit. The New Orleans group would take a loss on the inflated cottage prices, and that would offset taxes due on the condo sales. And the campus would get a condo neighbor nobody wanted or needed. I needed to keep it quiet, ask a few discreet questions, and determine how best to use it against Benjamin and others to stop the madness.

The final documents were three property deeds. Looking up the records, I found they were smaller plots along the ridge that adjoined the large acreage for the planned development. Joe had bought them from elderly or absentee landowners at a discount. From county tax records it seemed they were worth a few hundred thousand dollars, more if the development went through. Right now they were not worth much as they'd have to go through probate and might even be seized by creditors or other parties.

But I knew a guy. The kind that could easily falsify sales documents and forge deeds to show that Joe had recently sold them to another party. The same party to which I knew that Joe owed a large gambling debt to. The same one that would not be happy that Joe was dead and couldn't pay. Those deeds were going to Atlanta to keep me out of trouble since I was the cause of his death. A death I did not regret. Although it left some details unknown, such as who helped Joe move Tammy's car, or who else he was working with on the land deal. Some things I would likely never know.

Satisfied with my efforts, I drove toward home. But I had a stop to make at a storage facility in Manchester. I needed to meet a guy with a trailer.

I drove up to Millard's house in the afternoon. He was on the front porch giving me a hard look.

"James, have you gone crazy?"

"You mean crazier?"

"What is that thing? Looks like a golf cart made by NASCAR."

"That's an excellent description. Had this up in the mountains at a campground in the summer, then at the Asheville house the rest of the year. When the hurricane came through and messed everything up, this was the only way to get around for days with the roads blocked."

"Guess you don't need it down here."

"Glad you think that way."

"What do you mean?"

"Welcome to your new chariot."

"You must be kidding."

"No, I think you could use it and I don't need or want it."

"I guess I could use it to get around. Is it easy to drive?"

"Easier than a car. But it gets a little brisk in the wintertime. Lack of side windows and all."

"I bet. James, I want you to have my telescope. Take it in trade for this at least."

"That's a really nice scope, Millard. Besides, how can you see the lake without it?"

"Huh, I'll see the lake from up close. I'll drive this thing down there so no reason to use the scope on the porch."

"OK, you have a deal. And if there are any good night viewing events coming up, we can drive that thing to the old golf course and take the scope with us."

"Excellent, we will do that. You bring the snacks and I'll bring the liquor. Not sure I want to drink yours anymore."

"Oh, that reminds me, I ran this by Bryan. This is mostly street legal. You still have a license?"

"I do. For my old car in the garage I use sometimes to get groceries or go to the doctor."

"Good, you are cleared for campus. He also said you might get away with taking it into Warm Springs. Since there's not a town police department, they can't cite you, although the county deputies might."

"I can talk to the town council, maybe get a waiver for within the city limits."

"That's a good idea. You can get gas down there of course. Plus stop in at Mable's for the specials."

"Maybe I will. Thanks James, I really appreciate it."

"Happy to do it Millard. Now, let's go for a spin down to the lake. I think you'll have it mastered by the time we get there."

"Well, yeah, I had a go-cart when I was a kid. This thing is just a bigger version. Does it have seat belts? You better strap in."

We made it to the lake and back. Millard seemed happy

and I knew he could get around easier with it. My days of using it ended once the hurricane cleanup in Asheville was complete. Well, as complete as it was going to get. It was useful for the two weeks the roads were down. Now it was time to find it a new home. I walked back to the house and sat with Kat. She was happy after her snack and now only needed her belly rub.

It had been a long few weeks. I needed a break to work on the guest cottage and start thinking about what to remodel in the house. Manual labor, walks, and bike rides were my future. No more murder investigations to distract me.

Albert, my former UGA colleague called as I pulled into the driveway.

"Hello Al," I said. "How is it going?"

"I got your papers scanned and analyzed finally. Or rather, the student did."

"Oh good. I'd almost forgotten them."

"Then I'm glad I wasted the grad student's time and our lab resources for an important project you didn't even remember."

"Al, I appreciate you looking at those I really do. I owe you one. But it has been busy down here."

"Busy in Warm Springs? We must have different definitions of busy. Anyway, despite my gripes this was a fun project. What we found was unusual and most interesting. Historical too since it is dated 1945. Based on the ink and paper I'd say that is an accurate date. Unfortunately, it is completely out of context from anything we usually see. Maybe you can make some sense of it."

"I hope so. Was it a pound cake recipe?"

"Well, not exactly. Again, without context... I'm not sure. But it sounds like a murder confession."

The End

THANK YOU FOR READING. Please kindly consider leaving a rating or review. Read on for a preview for the next book in the series, Murder on Pine Mountain.

The Roosevelt Warm Springs, or RWS campus exists mostly as described. A few liberties were taken with details. For example, there is an abandoned camp on site by the lake, but it was not a Boy Scout retreat.

Similarly, the town of Warm Springs is mostly as described. Unfortunately, Mable's Diner does not exist and to my knowledge never has. Other restaurants and stores are there, however.

A significant change I made was to create the fictitious Hamilton County. It was carved from the actual counties of Meriwether, Harris, Troup and Talbot. The new county includes the towns of Warm Springs, Manchester, Pine Mountain, Shiloh, Woodland, and Hamilton, plus most of the ridge of Pine Mountain, and all of Roosevelt State Park. It was done to simplify jurisdictions of the towns, state park and RWS campus into one governmental entity. I made the county seat the town of Hamilton. It is a real county seat, but for Harris County.

The Roosevelt Warm Springs campus and the town of

Warm Springs are worth a visit, as well as the Little White House. All were amazing places in the time of Franklin D. Roosevelt, and hopefully RWS campus will be again.

Kat does exist and will welcome visitors. Kat is not her real name—I've used a pen name for her to protect her true identity. But if you see a fluffy tabico miniature Maine Coon cat eyeing chipmunks in front of the house, you'll know it's her.

ABOUT THE AUTHOR

I'm D. Smith, a native Georgian that can't seem to stay in the state for long. Tried a number of states and Europe so far, and lately have settled in Asheville, North Carolina. But I do now have a house on the Warm Springs Roosevelt campus, so soon that will be home.

I've been a lot of things over my work career, but I've put that nonsense behind me. The travel in America, Europe, and Asia was useful as an author. And finally the Ph.D. came in useful—for writing about food.

I now write books and pet cats for fun, since neither pays very well. I'm weaning myself away from social media, but the links below give a little more background and perhaps foreground on the author known as D. Smith.

RECIPE

APPLE DUTCH BABY OR GERMAN APPLE PANCAKE, SOUTHERN STYLE

This recipe is based on an old favorite and known by several names including Apple Dutch Baby or German Apple Pancake. It is reminiscent of a sweet version of Yorkshire Pudding, or popover, as the batter is similar, but without the beef drippings, of course. Also similar to but larger than Dutch Poffertjes. The dish gets a Southern kick by using drunken peaches rather than apple slices.

Batter

3 eggs

1/2 cup milk

1 teaspoon vanilla

1 tablespoon sugar

1/2 cup flour, all purpose (sifted if possible)

Add all but the four to mixing bowl and combine until smooth. Add flour. Use a blender or mixer to get the lumps out, or whisk longer if the flour is not sifted. Letting the milk and eggs warm to room temperature before mixing is recommended.

The batter can keep for a while. Cover and refrigerate

for a few minutes to a couple of days. Make the night before to save time.

Drunken Peaches

1 cup fresh sliced peaches

1/4 cup bourbon or rum

Slice the peaches less than a half inch thick. Thinner is fine but reduce cook time or you will end up with peach mush.

Soak overnight in bourbon, rum or spiced rum for less sweetness, or try Amaretto or Cointreau for more sweetness and flavor. If no alcohol is preferred, proceed to the cook step.

Use all if you are using a large skillet. Otherwise they will keep a couple of days in the refrigerator.

Any fruit will do, whether fresh or marinated. Cook fresh fruit, at least a cup, in the pan with butter and spices to caramelize. Feel free to experiment. Fresh apples and pears together make a nice fall mixture, blueberries for summer.

The Process

1/2 stick butter (4 tablespoons)

1/2 teaspoon cinnamon

1/4 teaspoon nutmeg

Melt butter in the skillet and add spices. Add peaches and cook on medium to get a slight caramel coating. I use 1 teaspoon speculoos (a Dutch spice blend) for the spice.

Once the fruit is cooked, pour in the batter and immediately place the skillet in the over, preheated to 425 F. Give it room above as the batter will balloon up off the skillet. Cook 15 minutes and check; don't over brown, just get the middle cooked.

Finishing Touches

Serve in the skillet or a large plate. Toss some confectioner's sugar or some raw brown sugar on top before eating. Depends on whether you want the powdered look or something with a little crunch. Or, for the sweetest tooth, both. For true decadence, drop fresh whipped cream on it.

Note: Most of my recipes are very loose as I frequently experiment and encourage others to do so. There are however some portions that can't be adjusted much without disaster ensuing. For this recipe, the batter should ingredients and steps should be kept. There are other versions of the batter if you research, but those should also be adhered to closely. The batter is the key to making a consistent and tasty pancake every time.

MURDER ON PINE MOUNTAIN

Chapter One

"Good morning hero." Lottie only called me that because she knew it irked me. But it was now part of our banter, so I didn't mind as much. I earned the label by solving a murder and accidentally killing the killer in my living room last spring.

"Hey Lottie."

"You wanting the usual?"

"No, this morning I'll take avocado toast with a side of roasted chia seeds and brie. And an algae smoothie with pickled quail eggs."

"Whatever that is, hero, you ain't getting it here. What you are getting is the usual."

"Thanks Lottie, that'll be just fine."

"You know it." She left to put the order in. I guess I should be honored that she considered me a regular. She wasn't as nice to new people. Mable's Diner was my go-to place a couple of times a week for breakfast or brunch in Warm Springs. I attended more often than in the past since my new business was next door.

She brought me a large biscuit filled with scrambled eggs, cheese, and bacon all melted together inside. I ate my customary half. The rest would be for lunch, mine plus some shared with my cat. Kat would demand a taste but would not eat much. I was also watching her cholesterol.

"You making any money next door?" Lottie asked, when she came by to refill my coffee.

"That would be a definite no."

"Not much of a mystery, hero. We don't exactly have an erudite populace hereabouts."

"Why Lottie, I didn't know you were a wordsmith."

"What you don't know would fill a search engine."

"Probably. But I'm still young enough to think I know everything."

She snorted and moved on. I went back to brooding on my latest endeavor. I had been getting bored in Warm Springs. A few months ago, a small retail space opened up in the same sprawling brick building that Mable's was in. I took over the lease and began what might be the worst idea I'd had in a while. Or the best, given enough time. It was a bookstore. Even if it wasn't profitable it gave me and Kat a place to go during the day.

Unfortunately, I didn't have many customers. Most came through to see Kat. Or were customers coming out of Mable's and needed some extra time to digest. I also got to see the huge dirty underbelly of the book world. I knew about that world from the other side, from writing non-fiction textbooks and historical fiction novels. But the initial business of running a bookstore was maddening. At least for me, at this early stage. Trying to decide what books to stock, whether ones I liked or bestsellers, to keeping up with inventory, and dealing with various wholesalers and publishers kept me busy in a bad way. I just wanted to sit in my bookstore with Kat and watch books fly off the shelves. I knew every new business startup was like this, feeling overwhelmed with new processes and being unprofitable. I was getting too old for this though.

It sounded so cool, owning a bookstore. Like owning a famous restaurant, or an established bed and breakfast. I should have known better. Every town should have a great bookstore, but someone besides me should own it. Same as swimming pools, horses, and airplanes. All things your best friend or neighbor owns but you get to play with without ownership responsibility. But it was something Emma and I had talked about semi-seriously for years. I knew I did not want the bed and breakfast or restaurant, but maybe we could have done a bookstore together. Except now I was doing it alone.

I was trying to make the store successful. Even before opening I had spent time thinking of different ways to bring in customers. I did it even more since opening, when the tedious details of the business allowed me time. Last week I scheduled a local author event. Donna Childers lived in the area and wrote romantic mystery under a pen name. She had come by and introduced herself. While she wandered around the store I checked and saw she was doing well enough online. Kat also followed her around, which was an important endorsement. I invited Donna to have a reading and book signing at the store. She agreed, and I did some advertising. Donna could meet some local fans and maybe I could move some books. It wasn't the worst way of marketing. Nor the worst way of getting to see Donna again.

Two days ago, on Saturday, Donna had arrived at the store. We were both full of hope. I helped her bring in a table and we set it up. She had a covering, a banner, her books, some freebies to give out, and a luscious silver platter of pastries. I did my best to be polite and not notice how attractive she was. She had long chestnut hair, bright blue eyes, and a mischievous smile. Which had nothing to do with her being the first author to present at the store.

Unfortunately, one of us, probably me, had forgotten to lock the table legs. An enthusiastic patron bumped the table… and just like that I had the first official book signing disaster at my store. Donna was great about everything and so were the customers. The remaining pastries hit the floor and some of the books got scuffed, but no major harm done. I was appalled but Donna kept on going without a skip. That was an admirable quality.

Donna commenced her reading as two dozen customers settled in their seats. Her writing was funny, and she had excellent timing and rhythm telling her stories. All the fans were entranced. Then the power went off.

I had some candles in the desk drawer, so she finished in candlelight, which wasn't the worst way to end a signing. I felt bad about the whole thing and offered to buy her dinner. She accepted, and we had plans to go to Woodbury on Friday night. Kat liked her so that was a positive.

Although it could have been all the pastry crumbs Kat got to eat off the floor after the table disaster. The little dustmop had developed a bit of a sweet tooth.

"Hey Romeo, where you taking Donna to eat?" Lottie roused from my remembrance.

"If you already know about the dinner, you should know the where."

"I heard Woodbury, but I know you know better than that."

"Uh, what?"

"That place ain't great. Donna's a class act. Do better, Romeo."

"OK, what would you suggest?"

"I heard you can cook. Why don't you cook for her?"

"That might be presumptuous."

"Nah, it's not a date. You just owe her for the fiasco you put her through."

"Lottie, you might just be the most vexatious person in this town."

"Why thank you, Romeo. That makes my day." If nothing else I at least had a new nickname. I wasn't sure it was better than hero though.

"Lottie, you aren't going to call me that in front of Donna, are you?"

"Nah, I don't want to raise her expectations too high."

"Thanks."

I paid the tab, put the half of a stuffed biscuit in a paper bag, and got a smirk from Lottie. Then I left for the long trip back to work. Perhaps fifty steps. I unlocked the door and turned to the sign on the door around to indicate the store was open. Now I had to worry about where to take

Donna on Friday or ask her over to my house. I was not good at this, and Lottie had realized it. Attacking the weakest animal in the herd, me. Well, time to be decisive and deal with it.

I called Donna and she answered. She was writing but ready to take a break. We made small talk for two minutes.

"Say Donna, instead of going to Woodbury on Friday, I'd like to offer the choice of coming to my house for dinner."

"James, I'd love to come over. The only cooked meals I get are my own and I'm about tired of my cooking."

"Great, and I know how you feel. Is there anything in particular you don't like? I'll make sure and leave it off the menu."

"No, nothing comes to mind. I'm sure whatever you come up with will be fine." Wonderful, that gave me nothing to go on. Chicken, seafood, steak? Pasta or salad? Vegetarian? I was going to have to wing it, pun intended. But I'd never serve wings on a date. Or a friendly get together.

"That sounds good. What time would you like to come over?"

"I'll be there around six."

"I'm on the Roosevelt campus if you remember."

"Yes, the house beside the police station. I know where it is."

"Great, see you then."

"I'm looking forward to it. Bye."

That went better than expected. Maybe Lottie was right. Now I was sitting in awe that I was surrounded by books at my bookstore. It made all the hassle worth it for a few moments. Followed by panic that I hadn't gotten the right orders in, or that the local and state taxes were incorrect. Then Kat sat by me and demanded some neck rubs. A customer came in and bought a book. I was fine again for a while. It must be shop owner regret or something.